FAMOUS CHILDREN

AND FAMISHED ADULTS

FAMOUS CHILDREN

AND FAMISHED ADULTS

STORIES

EVELYN HAMPTON

FC2

TUSCALOOSA

FC2 is an imprint of The University of Alabama Press
Inquiries about reproducing material from this work should be
addressed to The University of Alabama Press

Book Design: Publications Unit, Department of English, Illinois
    State University; Director: Steve Halle, Production Intern: Emi
    Howard
Cover Design: Lou Robinson
Typeface: Adobe Caslon Pro

Library of Congress Cataloging-in-Publication Data
Names: Hampton, Evelyn, author.
Title: Famous children and famished adults : stories / Evelyn Hampton.
Description: Tuscaloosa : FC2, [2019]
Identifiers: LCCN 2018041865 (print) | LCCN 2018042804 (ebook)
| ISBN
    9781573668804 (E-Book) | ISBN 9781573660693 (pbk.)
Classification: LCC PS3608.A69594 (ebook) | LCC PS3608.A69594
A6 2019 (print)
| DDC 813/.6—dc23
LC record available at https://lccn.loc.gov/2018041865

CONTENTS

FISHMAKER

Then I made fish.

I was living in the bank of a river. I'd found a small den and outfitted it simply.

I needed only a few things: work to do, a place where I could do it, and rest.

First I would decide on a design for a fish, then prepare the parts from a supply of materials I kept on shelves I'd built of wood dragged from the river.

The lining of a fish is a form of electricity.

A fish's brain can be made of almost anything, as long as it's small enough to fit inside the skull. A fish's skull can be made from windshield wiper fluid caps. These could be found in the river.

My favorite was plunging my hand into the sack of dry fish-eye lenses. The little pink ovals felt like sun-warm sand on a beach, a day of no worries. I knew the delight of a chef when finally her pantry is stocked only with the best ingredients—she can taste and touch and look at them, content that everything she makes will be delicious.

Brainstems are small white rods that become translucent as soon as they are attached to the lining.

When I ground the seeds for the paste I would cast teeth from, I added a pinch of white pepper from the shaker on my table.

On the basis of its ingredients, life shouldn't exist.

Making the eyes was a most delicate process. Sometimes, anticipating the demands of the work before me, my hands would shake so much, I wouldn't be able to take the rubber band off the bag of irises. They looked like brown mustard seeds and would take on the consistency of tapioca pearls when I placed them in eye fluid. I used a tweezers for this, after my hands had steadied.

For the blood I would make a kind of jelly. The stuff would visibly hiss when I added the final ingredient, a dash of sea salt I'd brought with me from the city.

I had lived so many different lives in so many different places, the sight of the salt shaker, this little container of crystals, gave me such comfort—seeing it day after day on its shelf was like seeing the face of a dear one who had aged gently beside me.

I liked to think of that hiss as the fish's first breath. It wasn't a sound of relief but of shock and discomfort. Life must be surprised to be so suddenly embodied.

I am old, let it be no mystery. I'm older than walls and most days I feel stiffer than a brick.

Something I learned making fish is that life isn't very good at living—it has to be coaxed and prodded to take to its next body.

And then even after it has taken and gives every sign of being a success, life tends to remain limp and dormant.

Anyone who has lived in a winter climate and watched snow falling on the first day of May knows how very far away life can get from the ones craving it.

I am so old now, I keep my skin in a zipped bag in the refrigerator. It stays fresher longer; when I put it on, I like how cool I feel, almost as if I am young again. The coolness of my skin during those first minutes out of the refrigerator reminds me of the walls of the den. Those were happy days, making fish. Even my shadow was content.

In the outer wall, I'd made a hatch to throw finished fish out of, into the river. The hatch also functioned as a window for me. I liked a certain kind of light.

It would frighten me to look into a fish's eyes the moment before I threw it out of the hatch. I would see there a dilating terror that encompassed everything. Was it knowledge?

How had knowledge gotten into the fish? I hadn't put it there. Knowledge wasn't one of the ingredients. Consciousness, never.

Usually there would be a tomcat crouched in the hatch. The look in a fish's eyes told me it already knew this cat, had seen it a hundred times, had been caught and eaten by it in lifetimes past. *Please don't throw me out of that hatch!*, its eyes were pleading.

But I always threw the fish out. I wasn't going to spare them from what they knew was coming. I had made them—I was much worse than that tomcat.

They should have been relieved to be tossed out of the hatch. To escape their maker—their death.

At first I resented that tomcat gobbling up my careful handiwork.

But when I watched with an attitude a little more detached than disdainful, I noticed that not every fish got caught. Only the ones life hadn't really taken to were gobbled. The ones in which life was vigorous thrashed their tails and flipped their bodies and managed to evade old Tomcat.

These fish made it into the river, where other perils worse than Tomcat awaited. The other fish, the weak ones Tomcat caught, would not have survived anyway. They were pretty fish, and exacting to make, but they were not hardy enough to be real.

In time I considered Tomcat my co-creator. His job was to test the final product.

I mentioned I liked a certain kind of light.

Indirect, reflected. The hatch let in sunlight reflected by the river. On my ceiling I could see the water's surface eddying and flowing its shadows.

Lucky me. Nobody from my old lives knew where to find me. I called myself Lucky.

Old lovers, old loves; debts and family: they had exhausted all my old haunts. I was relieved to have finally been forgotten.

Being alive is mostly a matter of believing you're alive.

Once their eyes were attached to the lining, the fish could see. Once they could see, they could believe. They blinked and blinked.

The air in my den was cool and damp, excellent for naps.

Before I became Lucky, I was no good at sleeping. I just couldn't find the right time or position. I wandered restlessly, searching for relief.

When you're happy, sleeping is easy. Counterintuitive maybe, but when you're happy, it's easier to leave your life. Relaxed, you can slip right out of it. You can always come back to it later, and if you can't, no big deal.

Maybe it's a matter of having proper lighting, happiness. Light should not impede the ascension of dreams.

Yet one day it did. Happy, I was lying on my back, preparing for a nap. I gazed up at the ceiling, and instead of riverlight flowing past, I saw a brittle, jagged kind of light, more knife than light. I could not look at it without feeling as if my teeth were going to crumble right then and fall out of my head.

Lucky I have been, and Lucky I no longer am, I thought.

I went to the hatch and looked down at the river.

So long, easy sleep. Goodbye happiness.

River? No. That mass of cracks was not what a river was.

Time to find new names for everything. *Despair. Apocalypse.* Old Tomcat yowled. He hissed. He moaned. He grunted. He lay down on the ledge outside the hatch and let loose a litter of kittens.

So. Old Tomcat was neither Old nor Tomcat. Figured. She would need a new name too.

And these mewling things beside her, they would need names. She licked their heads between their blind eyes. She laid her head back and let them feed on her milky body.

Below were the broken bones of what used to be called River.

Despair, I named the kitten with a white stripe between black eyes. Apocalypse, I named the one that looked vaguely at me. Two-Headed, Nobody, and Sheila were the other three.

I fed Not-Old-Not-Tomcat some of my fish ingredients. She ate them scavengingly while Despair, Apocalypse, Two-Headed, Nobody, and Sheila mewled and sucked on her. *Not*, I shortened her name to. She seemed to have diminished considerably from her Old Tomcat days.

I called myself Un. The Undoer. Undone.

Not ate the eyes one at a time. I let my hand reach out and pat her head. She ate a few brainstems.

My thoughts turned then to the ocean.

+

Sometimes things just dry up—that might make a nice, stupid ending.

Not,

Despair,

Apocalypse,

Two-Headed,

Nobody,

Sheila,

and me, Un. We were a company.

In my den our business was doing nothing. Making nothing. Going nowhere.

The cracks in the mud of the river sometimes looked at me. Sizing me up. *Why don't you come with us*, they said in a masked voice coming from somewhere under the cracked earth. *Sometimes things just dry up.*

Get over it.

Two-Headed developed a strain of apathy that made him want to devour me.

He would sleep on my neck. Always this led to chewing. Even his dreams were hungry. Well, so were mine, when I managed to have one.

I sprinkled fish scales on the rug when I wanted to see pure appetite's teeth. Pure appetite's claws. Quite a lot of cat blood was shed because of my boredom.

Two-Headed always got the most of whatever it was. I named him Chief Executive Officer of Discorporation.

I made a little sign. Wrote it in cat's blood, hung it above the door to the den. DISCORPORATION.

Things were becoming squalid. Things were, shall we say, in a state of drastic decline.

The cracks would laugh sometimes. *Why don't you . . .* they said one morning. Their voice sounded like a platter heaped with pancakes dripping with syrup. *Help us, Un,* they dripped. Only, the syrup was blood.

As a souvenir, I kept a little bit of fish lining in a small glass box. Blue sparks still shot through the lining. I would watch them through the walls of the box. At night I would hear crackling like the static between radio stations. It was the lining, searching for a body to light with life.

How about a song, I would hear a voice within the lining ask itself. This would be in the middle of the night. The cats of

Discorporation around me howling in their sleep. *This one goes out to . . .* and then the static would begin crackling again, this time to a different rhythm.

The fact that Two-Headed actually had two heads did not change anything.

I imagine the lining of an antelope or a dog would behave in much the same way fish lining did.

I could not have been a maker of mountain lions or of humans—I only cared about making fish.

The lining of a hawk—it would make an elegant jacket. Dark and fitted.

I am old, but I still consider the possibilities.

Though mostly what I do is look back, I still see:

Sometimes there's even someone new coming toward me.

Who will she be this time? Or he. Long nights, little sleep—I'll take just about anything. Even if it's only my own past coming back. (There is only so much future. Only so much raw material for time to make its designs upon.)

Sheila was becoming more and more stunning. One of those objects which exist only once they have disappeared. Her fur had begun to shimmer. Colors undulated along her back. Would not let me pet her. Crouched all day at the hatch looking down. Did not even come down to fight Two-Headed for a bit of brain.

The less she behaved like a cat, the more stunningly beautiful she became.

Suspicious, Two-Headed would hiss at her. She was not being enough of a cat to satisfy him.

Look at me, she said one morning.

I was still in bed, static lining my drowse with its shifting frequencies.

I looked toward the hatch. I had recognized the voice as Sheila's. It sounded exactly the way I expected Sheila to sound, like a piece of purple velvet wrapped around sunflower seeds, tied off with jute thread.

Look down, Sheila's voice said.

There in the riverbed sat an old boat, decrepit, DELIVER-ANCE in faded paint on its keel.

A woman sat in the captain's nest. Hair black as it gets. Purple shimmer wafting off the waves of its hanks.

Later I was not surprised to find that the lining had been lifted from my little glass box. Its lid had been tipped open. Only a few shreds of the lining were left. The work—I would recognize it in my sleep—of a cat's teeth. Sheila.

She turned a key; the rudder sputtered. I saw the boat had tires.

All aboard, Sheila said.

+

That's how we got to the ocean. Sheila drove.

When we arrived, we rented a little cabin on the beach. BEACHCOMBERS PARADISE said the sign. The owners hadn't made the S possessive. Paradise belonged to nobody.

Which reminds me—Nobody hadn't made it. He'd leaped from Deliverance and took off into the forest with Apocalypse. Not, Two-Headed, Despair, Sheila, and me, Un—we were the only occupants of Paradise. It was the off-season.

Apparently other people were not interested in seeing how towering the waves can be in January.

They want sunsets, Mel said. Mel was one of the caretakers of Paradise. The other was Holly. She was ill; dying, Mel said. They'd come here so she could do it in peace.

I asked why we never saw Holly at the beach. Was she too sick even to sit?

Doesn't like to see the horizon anymore, Mel said. It makes her queasy. Ceiling and feet—those are the things she likes to see now. If you come to visit wear nice shoes, she'll appreciate it.

+

I spent days walking the beach. It is essentially a boneyard, the beach, a vast cemetery. It comforted me to be surrounded by so many possibilities. I began scheming about how I could use these washed-up pieces of life, maybe make fish again . . .

I would look out at the horizon, wondering how many of *my* fish had made it that far.

Mine—I still thought of them that way.

The horizon is made of pure wondering, by the way. We make it distant merely by longing for it, since longing pushes away its object at the same time it reaches for it.

Sheila mostly stayed in the cabin with the cats, fiddling with lids and tea. At night we would sit together on the deck, our bodies almost touching. I would feel the crackle of the lining leaping between us, arc of energy. I wondered how long it would be before we . . .

We should visit Holly, Sheila said one night.

We?

The woman's dying, and we haven't visited yet.

Ok, say hi for me, I said. I was frightened of Holly. No, I was frightened of death. Death had nothing to do with Holly, nothing to do with anything at all; it was impersonal, that's what frightened me about it. No name can keep it away.

The crackle of the lining I liked. Even the hiss of the fish. The look in their eyes as they began to live. Life—I craved it. I wanted to make more and more of it. Gather together all the fragments on the beach, make something that would be able to see me.

The life in another's eyes verified my life. But death, it took me away from me.

No, we should both go. Out of respect. For Mel. Think of what he must be going through.

I imagined Mel actually passing through something, Holly's death a dark corridor, Mel blinking and crawling through it.

We knocked on the door of their cabin the next morning.

Mel's face was no longer Mel's face; it belonged to gray, like a soft, unappetizing cheese.

We brought you something, said Sheila as Mel let us in. I thought, *We did?* I didn't recall bringing anything. Yet I watched as Sheila pulled it from her pocket—the fish lining. *My* fish lining, from my little glass box. She hadn't devoured it after all. She'd been keeping it with us, and from me.

As she handed it to Mel, blue sparks fell to the floor and crackled for a moment at our feet like sparklers, then went quiet. In his hand the lining danced and laughed and leapt and threw flickers of blue into the room. I thought of the river again, its surface reflected on the ceiling of my den.

She'll love it, said Mel. Thank you.

He unfolded it, then folded it, then put it in his shirt pocket. I'll introduce you to Holly, he said.

We followed him to the bedroom. I hoped that when he opened the door, the room would be empty except for a chest of drawers made of dark, deeply grained wood, the kind that captures light and gives the impression that it contains all of space in its surface. Each drawer would be a different size. *This is Holly*, Mel would say. He would open a drawer; inside, a blue marble. In another drawer, a wind-up eye. In another, one of those birds that endlessly dips its head to drink water from a dish. In another drawer, another, smaller drawer, taking me farther from reality . . .

Instead what we saw in the bedroom was a bed, and on it a woman, a real, dying one. I knew she was dying by her breath—it could hardly lift itself out of her body anymore, and the look in Holly's eyes seemed to be falling inward towards it. I had watched this happen with the fish: as they died they would disappear into their own eyes.

Scattered on the floor around her were yellow tissues, books, dishes that must have held Mel's meals so that he never had to leave her side.

Come in, Holly said when she saw us. She smiled a little and didn't lift her head off the pillow.

Mel introduced us as *our guests*, which I could tell he immediately regretted because Holly's face drew into itself and she said, I'm sorry there's such a mess.

We're not that kind of guest, Sheila said. She smiled. She knew how to have the right effect. Holly smiled and Mel said, They brought you a gift.

Oh! said Holly. I love gifts.

When we left, Holly's eyes were shut. The square of lining flickered in one of her hands.

+

Late that night, Sheila and I sat on the deck of our cabin. I was waiting for her to lift one of her hands to the back of my neck, which tonight felt too exposed. I knew the movement was coming; I could feel it weighing itself between us, making the air around our mouths ready. When we breathed, the readiness entered our heads. *Now, Sheila,* I was thinking. *Now is the time to touch me please.*

Sheila lifted one of her hands, placed it on my knee. Are you mad? she asked. I gave away your lining.

Stole it, then gave it away, I said. I tried to laugh, laughed a little. After you did away with one of my cats.

I didn't make the river dry up, at least. That one wasn't my fault.

I could feel the air crinkling around her smile, touching her teeth.

Her hand was still on my knee. The weight of it on my body kept answering her question. Was I mad? Keep touching me.

Sheila, I said.

At night there's no horizon; or it's so near, everything exists within it. We walked through the boneyard of the beach and at a point in the night that had no depth, we slept.

+

In the morning, Mel stood on our deck. His face still belonged to gray, but there was relief around his chest. Holly was dead. She had died during the night. I could tell he was breathing better now that death had left that room. Even though it had left by way of Holly.

I wanted to invite you to Holly's funeral, he said. It'll just be us. Her body's already on the boat. He gestured toward something between the back of his shirt and the horizon. Floating there was a red boat about the size of Deliverance, but eminently more seaworthy, to judge by the fact that it could actually float.

In it, Holly lay on a simple straw mat, her hands resting alongside her nightgown, inside of which her body seemed to have faded to a flat white line. Sheila and I sat on benches around her while Mel navigated.

Do you want this back? he asked once he'd stilled the engine and we were floating with the current. He'd taken us far from the beach—no more cabins, no more land. The bottom of the boat was the only sure footing, and it was never still.

He took the lining out of a pocket of his jacket. When she died it was in her hand, he said.

No, it should go with Holly, Sheila said. She looked at me. The look told me that I agreed.

Mel nodded, tucked it into Holly's nightgown. We helped him lift Holly over the starboard side of the hull. There wasn't any pause or ceremony—once we had her up we let her drop into the water. Splash.

Or rather the entire thing was ceremony—the water, its buoyancy, us floating upon it.

ADORED, OR RED

They climb in through her window, or when her parents are gone, they moonwalk and Roger Rabbit through her front door. They want to use toilets, bend swabs into their ears, wrap gauze around their faces and sink like they've been punched into the leather of her couch. Punching buttons, opening doors, they ask, How many clocks? How many clocks do your parents need to own? And then they are surprised by how much time has passed since whenever. Since food, since fucking. Since last Saturday in Phoenix, since Sunday supper in the free kitchen, since someone recognized them as familiar.

She is in love with one of them. His friends are like his clothes: smelly, weirdly matted on one side, faded on the other from hanging out too long in the sun in one position. She lets them all in when nobody's home. This is after school. During school, she fools everyone. They believe she wants to go to a good college.

Nobody wants us, they tell her. She lets them in, and in further, into her parents' bed, even. She wants the one she's in love with to see her bending forward over the counter in the kitchen, so she says, Let's make a cake!

K, whatever, they say, trailing their ripped pant legs after. They think she is like some Tinsel, an over-sweet drink they had once after an after-party that made everybody feel like they were made of plastic.

The one she is in love with plucks a sunfish from her mom's aquarium and makes its tiny lips move with his fingers, saying with his high-pitched voice pitched higher, I drive a Cadillac. He tosses it back in the tank. The fish swims in tighter and tighter circles, then sinks with its belly up.

She says, Doesn't matter, don't worry.

I'm going to major in history, she says when any adult asks her. *They* never ask. Pierced tongues, electrified hair, rangy in their glances, they appear outside her bedroom window and tap two times, three if she's asleep, and mouth her name, making fog appear in halos around their faces.

Who are you, a new one asks her. She shrugs. She lets him in, lets them all come in. She says a name that hangs around her throat like music, the S the treble clef for ARAH. She still plays the flute in eleventh grade. She's quiet as air rising from a cake. The one she's in love with tells her, Get some balls. Her father is a golfer. Her parents have some money. She wants to hide this but doesn't know where. She wears gold earrings; they wear safety pins. She shows them his clubs and poses. They seem bored. They pose on the couch in matching slouches.

They watch *Mallrats* on her mother's rug from India. They ask when her parents will leave the continent again. They put their heads in doors and say, Food, God, I'm hungry.

They are named after cities, after states where they say they came from or were born into: Coma, Tex, Gary, Cincinnati, Weed, Madison.

They ask her, Where were you born?

Money, one says. A kind of island.

Right there, she says, and points to the faint stain beside the love seat.

Love, they call her, what's it like to have money? What's it like to have a mattress, to have a golden name?

The one she's in love with stays late after the others have shuffled across the backyard, away under her old swing set. He writes his name in capitals on her arms in black Sharpie. She met him at her parents' yard sale; he and his friends came and broke an antique clock, said they were looking for cheap vinyl, named specific names she'd never heard of.

Next, she invited them inside.

Next, her parents were leaving on a twenty-day tour of other rich peoples' houses.

Next, the one she's in love with was a week without leaving, stealing from her parents with one hand in her back pocket. She was putting on her mother's lipstick, a color called Adored, Or Red.

Next, he and she were listening to "Modern Love" and fucking on a Persian rug really from Portland.

Next, Turn that fucking thing off, someone said when they got home.

BB AND CALLA LILY

That was the night we got older. Momma had just been canned. We were going up to the Dairy Land when Calla Lily asked, Don't you think we should bring Thomas. Thomas was our dad. He was not our father, but he was in the position of the man, having been married to Momma for a few weeks. Funny about their wedding—nobody came because the invitation said the wrong day. It said the right day, but Momma and Thomas got fidgety and went ahead with it a day before the day, like time wasn't for them, only for the RSVP'd. The folks did come, but there was no gown for them to see, and no aisle, and no Momma and no Thomas—me and Calla Lily had to tell everybody that, see, they had gone to Thomas's parents', sort of, or that's what they said to say, because they had already done the wedding. I hate being looked at like that by so many relations I never see, it's like the air itself suddenly lays claim to me, wasps flown from a falling tree. We didn't hear of them again, the RSVP'd, and a few days later Momma and Thomas came back to time and asked had we eaten. Took us out for supper, me and Calla Lily, ate our favorite chicken. Creamed.

Back to the trip up to Dairy Land. Momma was on a jag after being canned. Thomas had gone all weary and got a strange look on him, laying all day on the creeping pattern of the couch that looks like it's moving when you're not looking at it, then you look at it direct and it stops creeping, then you look away and it creeps again. That's how Thomas lay.

Pick him up, just—throw him in the trunk? Calla Lily was like a murderer with all the tough taken away, and all the hate. She had these ideas that made you think, *Now that's going to get us put away.* And prison was never far from where we were living. But she didn't mean it to be mean, she just meant—I don't know, to be nice or something. She wanted Thomas to have a shake. Calla Lily always got peanut butter banana, the flavor preferred by murderers who aren't murderers, I read somewhere. I got something different every time, they have so many flavors at the Dairy Land, you never get tired. You always get a shake.

So Thomas wasn't moving much when we picked him off the creeping couch, carried him into the trunk. Why not the back seat? That's the question I asked Calla Lily, but she couldn't see it that way. She couldn't see us driving up to Dairy Land, Momma off on a jag, with Thomas in the back seat. Just couldn't see it that way. A shortage in the brain, had Calla Lily. Too fast a metabolism. A mind sometimes like the object of her name, pretty and petalled and just a thing for the bees and sunshine to sway. Just couldn't imagine Thomas being able to lay in the back seat while me and Calla Lily was driving up that way, to the Dairy Land, where you never had to have the same flavor, they had so many, but Calla Lily always got the same. Because, she had a shortage, in the brain. Just a white curl in a green field was Calla Lily's mind sometimes.

But Calla Lily, I said, I *can* see it that way, and what I see is this: you and me driving up the Dairy Land, some cop coming along the highway like a lurch, you and me pulling over because, well, no because, just—and cop shining his light, or maybe he'll be a her, shining her light in the back seat and seeing Thomas there asleep, no trouble, just a man fallen asleep on the drive home, we have to drive our daddy back, no questions, nothing to ask, maybe he even gives us a nickel, or she. But you and me driving and Thomas *not* in the back seat, and cop shining her light all around the emptiness, it'll put a thing in her brain, like a worm, and she'll think, or maybe she'll be a he, he'll think, *I've got to see in the trunk.* That's what the worm in his brain will say, and you know how cops do whatever the worms in their brains tell them to, and pretty soon we'll be having to pop the trunk, and that light will be shining, Calla Lily, right on Thomas's face, which looks so strange, soon it'll creep like the vines of the couch.

But Calla Lily just couldn't see it that way. Just couldn't, even after she'd put a stick of watermelon Extra in her mouth and chewed it some. No, she said, we'll just put him in the trunk. When we get to Dairy Land we'll let him look about. We'll get him a shake. Momma being away, we'll just put Thomas in the trunk.

I suppose she never could see it that way, the way that would've kept us from getting older that night, for sometimes you can be seen by the authorities as adults even when you are not so aged. We put Thomas in the trunk and Calla

Lily and I both drove, we knew how to do it that way, me using my feet and Calla Lily looking and steering, the two of us together like the old cherry tree that was split by lightning, then grew as two trees, twining round the wound where they had been separated. I suppose we had our wound, me and Calla Lily, and our wound was away on a jag. And Thomas on the creeping couch, and the creeping couch. We ought to have scorched that pattern, or sewed like a coverlet, while Momma was away, instead of going out for a shake.

And, sure enough comes the cop. I saw the red flashing even from the floor where I was. But Calla Lily didn't see it that way. I'm not stopping, she said, though it was me who had the say, since I was on the pedals.

Oh yes, I said, you are. We.

I'm going to Dairy Land, she said, I'm already there with my shake. She was still chewing the Extra and had a bubble as big as her face.

I should have just pressed the brake. It would've been me who would've done it, but I didn't, so it became nobody's mistake. Between me and Calla Lily, it was nobody driving that car then. Just like if you looked direct at the creeping the creeping would go away, when I looked direct at who was driving I could see no driving, just me and Calla Lily in the stillness of being one wound together in a way.

THREE STORIES ABOUT MY MOTHER

PEARL, MY MOTHER

My mother's name is not Pearl. It is Maria. Sometimes people who know her call her Mary, like the Virgin. My mother is not a virgin. She is my mother. My father put his dick in her and made me. Later his dick in her made my brother. My brother is named after a saint. I am named after a real-life prostitute. Are there any saints who were prostitutes? Some people used to be named Dick, but not anymore. One of my favorite old names is Pearl. Once, my mother gave me a pearl necklace. She had only one pearl necklace, so she could only give it to me once. People make a big deal out of eating oysters because they are like little vaginas (the oysters, I mean). People slurp the oysters down into their throats and feel about themselves that they are capable of great fucking. The truth is, not many people are. Greatness is a rare thing, like a natural pearl. An oyster forms a pearl in response to irritation. Something unwanted gets into its shell, and the oyster envelops it, to make it more like itself. Then people kill the oysters and steal their pearls. People say that I have my mother's eyes, but she hasn't given me her eyes yet. They are still in her skull, looking out at the world with dismay.

WATERFALLS, WOLF

My parents are growing old. My father has waterfalls in his eyes now, and my mother is becoming a wolf.

The waterfalls cloud my father's vision and roar in his ears, so that he sees us only dimly, through a white mist, and hears what we say only faintly, through the sound of water crashing on the rocks below. His doctor says that we must not allow him to drive, he is dangerous.

I wonder whether, in our father's eyes, my brother and I look like tourists gawking at the sublime magnificence of the falls, while he, our father, sits behind a white curtain of flowing water, a sage in his redoubt?

By shouting, we manage to communicate to him that there is a surgery scheduled. He says he does not want to have the surgery, he does not want to be so exposed.

My mother is lucky, her rheumatologist says. The disease that is transforming her into a wolf was late in her case—often women are much younger when they experience their first symptom, a mask-like rash across the nose, cheeks, and eyes. But the disease is more virulent in aging bodies, so that the few extra years of youth its late onset gave her are now quickly being overtaken by troubling symptoms, such as insomnia and an extreme sensitivity to sunlight. She rarely goes outside during the day. When she does, she wears a hat with a wide, dark brim, and sunglasses, and she makes a deliberate effort to stay always in the shade.

She is also becoming more ruthless, because of a new keenness in her senses. Not infrequently she turns on me before I have opened my mouth and contradicts whatever I was about to suggest, as if she smells everything far in advance of its occurrence.

Though their maladies differ, in their senescence both my mother and father are similarly wary of exposure—my father to the sights and sounds of this world, and my mother to its sun.

Both conditions are hereditary, and I am already experiencing some of their symptoms. At 34, my eyes sometimes trouble me, and I have to put down the book I am reading or look away from the screen and stare into something called the *middle distance* in order to give my eyes a rest. In the last five years I have moved several times, each time farther north into the mountains, where the air is cool and fresh. My brother is lucky; he reads for hours without needing to look up from the page or screen, and he runs on the flat sidewalks of the large city where he lives at the hour when the day is brightest and hottest, when the concrete is so white it is blinding.

FOXES

One day the queen shocked her subjects by appearing before them much earlier than expected. The gathering became silent and ashamed.

When the queen saw the peculiar look of horror and adulation on the faces of her subjects, she said, "What unusual sympathies you people have!"

She was wearing a garment nobody had seen before: both green and scintillating, it proved easier to imagine than to see, so her subjects shut their eyes and dreamed.

Of course, its purpose was to deter foxes.

FROM DOCUMENTARY FILMMAKER JURGEN GROSSBINGER'S JOURNAL

6/8

We are now in the jungle. What is the jungle? We have not eaten anything in weeks except the insects that happen to fly unwittingly into our teeth. The insects we eat are fat with our own blood still warm from our bodies. Slowly we are devouring ourselves. That is the jungle.

Outside my tent a man-dog is barking at a tree. I do not know what a man-dog is. It looks like a hippopotamus.

6/9

I feel like a javelina salesman. Nobody wants anything to do with me. When I approach village leaders with the useless dollars in my outstretched hands, they run and hide. They stay so well hidden, I think they have turned into the trees from which a kind of rock-hard fruit falls on us. I had thought the fruit was mango but my guide tells me no, it is deadly poison, though its flesh be sweet.

Before, when one of the women saw me, she would gesture at her crotch with a motion like she was pulling a weed with a long taproot. The people here eat a diet rich in breads made from dried roots they harvest from the forest. But now the women do not even gesture at me—they run straightaway and hide. I am a monster. I speak a language, but language is not enough. I ought to speak an antidote to that fruit's poisonous flesh, a fruit with even sweeter flesh that is not poisonous.

Today on the road I met a fresh cow patty. Its sides were steep. Nevertheless I summited.

6/11

In the jungle, few days have passed since the beginning of time. The band of my watch has rotted to the flesh of my wrist. Slowly the timepiece is devouring my body. My shadow looks like a dinosaur's erection. Huge, thick leaves slap at my face like a granny. They tell me to eat, fatten up, look how thin I'm getting. Everything is preparing to eat me, who is not accustomed to vegetation dominating a man's flesh.

Tonight one of the camera operators died. Cause unknown. Already her body is in an advanced stage of decomposing. Did she have a family? The jungle devours givens, knowns.

6/12

Elsewhere, today is my birthday. In the jungle nobody was ever born. Carnivorous flowers defecate men. The sky is a stench. Babies have old-man faces. Babies are bestowed on mothers by snakes. Today I was bitten by our hired guide, whose name means *wait*. Tomorrow I will wait for death with renewed strength.

6/14

I no longer know the purpose of life. Is it to tell me that over there is a tree filled with vipers? Is it a dull rhythm being pounded out on a tin of peaches by a boy whose eyes revolve like stones when they look at me? I offered the boy some money for the peaches. He hissed.

Today I often said *forest* to myself. Truth itself wanders through the forest.

6/16

I want to say that soon we will finish filming, but in truth filming has not yet begun. Nothing has yet begun in the jungle. There is not yet an origin we can pin this madness on. If there were an origin, man would piss on it. I would piss on it.

Another camera operator has developed signs of dying. I am thinking of calling the disk jockey of my favorite radio show, which I have not heard in at least thirty years. I want to ask him to play a song by Stevie Wonder.

Later—

We would like to believe that in the absence of a map we can find the North Star and thereby figure out which way we are facing. But man is directionless. When I close my eyes all I can see are the backs of my teeth. They are filled with the openings of dark caves. I am sure I recognize the shape of one of the openings. It is the place in the Himalayas where a woman served me tea made with yak's milk, a fatty yellowish substance that tasted somehow of fish.

6/17

Today we finished building the ship that will carry Gustav down the river to the passage over the mountain. The ship is enormous. When it is before me it looks like a wall that rises up to and through the sky, and it extends as far as I can see to either side. A wall that nowhere has an end—I find the thought so comforting. Because there is no way to film such a thing. And because we will find a way.

6/18
The moon knows it is better off without the jungle, so it does not give even a little of its full light to us. Instead there is a stench—the night. It is when people close their eyes and try to have a dream.

I cannot close my eyes. My eyeballs are too dry. This is because of the tiny bugs that crawl into my eyes and suck them as if they were melons. I would do anything to suck on a melon, but there is nothing I can do, the jungle drains every effort of its effects. It is a parasite an order of magnitude larger than the ones sucking on my eyes. If only I were one of the bugs.

The doctor of our crew has not known what to do since we arrived here. He behaves like a man whose brain is being parasitized by one of the suckers that affix themselves to any sort of flesh with their hundreds of razor-sharp teeth. "They join their blood to your blood," explained our guide.

Airborne barracudas.

Turkey vultures, their eyes totally white, their talons dripping with organ meat.

This morning our guide told us about "the lurking jaguar." He says it is a legend that becomes real at least once during every man's life.

6/20

Tomorrow Gustav will arrive by helicopter, god willing. Everyone warns us that he has shed the last tatters of sanity like a snake its final skin. In fact, there is a snake in my cabin now in the process of molting. Occasionally it lunges at the end of its body that is still wrapped in its old flesh. This fellow will show no mercy to anybody, even itself. I must find a way to get it out of here. But everyone is sleeping like lousy dogs out in the open, twitching because of the bugs that feed on their flesh.

Our guide is off on a bender, I saw him yesterday, he was soaked with piss. Drunkenly he told me that his wife had died the night before, having been dragged from their bed by men with spears for teeth. He said he recognized one of the men, it was his brother.

Even the doctor twitches in his sleep like an old sow. Maybe I am starting to sympathize with the bugs. They have no mind, only an endless capacity for sucking man's blood.

6/21

Gustav arrived. He is clearly in the grip of a mania, it is at his mind like a demented hound. Yet he speaks like a poet. Thank god for Gustav. He brings exactly the sort of clarity the jungle needs: absolute madness. He believes staunchly, violently, that he is quite sound in mind and body, that it is we who are mad. No doubt he is correct.

I keep thinking of the young girl whom I once met on the road in a northern country. I had been traveling alone on foot, sleeping in abandoned shacks and houses that I managed to break into, trying to get to a hospital in Paris where my friend was dying. The girl asked me if I wanted to see something a little ways off the road in the woods. I declined her invitation.

I arrived at the hospital just in time to see the breathing tube being removed from my friend's mouth. She had just died. I was too late to say goodbye. I gently pulled her eyelids closed. The doctors had left her staring up into the abyss of the ceiling, where the useless hospital monitors still beeped and clicked like birds on the Isle of Diminishment.

Tonight I wish desperately that I would have accepted the girl's invitation.

6/23
Late this morning Gustav approached me with a wild look jutting out of his eyes. He told me that he had been bushwhacking in the jungle (I do not know what he meant, "bushwhacking"—no doubt something insane) when he came across a door. Just a door, an ordinary door resting on its hinges. He said they were metal and not rusted like one would expect. He said that he had tried to open the door and could not, it was apparently locked.

It is impossible that you saw a door, I told Gustav.

He insisted that what he had seen was a door.

It is impossible, I told him.

He said that he would show me the door.

I told him that he had better show me the door right away. I became enraged thinking of it. It didn't make sense. A gaping hole in the jungle—that makes sense. Rifts in time and coherence—those make sense, they exist in the jungle. But a door—no. The jungle plays tricks on your senses. It's full of lies, dreams, illusions. I have learned to tell the difference. My eyesight isn't perfect, but I can't be tricked.

We must have been walking for several hours when Gustav began to keen like an ape lamenting its dead. He was inhuman for several minutes, the time it takes a person to shit. But we were granted a reason for persisting in this doomed business—when Gustav quieted down, there it was, a sure thing, no lie: a door.

I can't say what the meaning of it is, why it has appeared here, now, at a time when I am most desperate for the last trappings of Western reality—money, cooperation among equals, a sense of progress. The door is certainly locked. The knob does not turn. Yet one can step to either side of it and knock, and nobody will answer.

It is as if we have encountered an object of someone else's dream.

It is just another gaping hole, I told Gustav.

Later, this thought: I hope it is the door to Madam. I had not thought of Madam for years, not since I last encountered her in Minsk. I had been doing some work for a porcelain artist—I was just out of school, working as a nude model. Maybe because of the rigors of maintaining an awkward position for hours, on a day when I was particularly susceptible to a notion I had then about reality, I began to feel more and more as if I was surrounded by a supremely strange organism—not a thing, but rather a sentient space of relations among all things. It introduced itself to me, though it did not speak, as Madam.

I despise men who *seek*, but what happened to me was undeniable, and undeniably I am now a man who seeks. I seek another experience like that one, another encounter with Madam. I want one more, the last one, so that I can cure myself of the first and return to being a man who does not seek.

By now the band of my watch is indistinguishable from the skin of my wrist. It appears that the gold-plated timepiece is growing from my flesh. The hands of the timepiece are sensitive nerve endings that leap whenever a mechanical signal tells them to do so.

6/24

Filming delayed. No Gustav. We have looked everywhere. I spread the cheeks of the ass of every dog I could find and looked in there for my friend. The dogs all have terrible mange. My hands itch. I will kill Gustav when I find him. No, first I will make him finish filming. Then I will kill him. I know he's gone back to that door. Nothing but a gaping, shrieking hole in that man where in other men there is a mind. That is why he is so great, and why I must find him and force him to finish this film. He is the only actor who I believe truly understands the plight of a man determined to haul a ship over a mountain. I don't understand the plight of such a man, and I am him.

If he has gone through that door, then I must also go through that door. Beyond it, will I find the realm of encounter?

Later—
I had wanted to make a picture of before the beginning: a river flowing ceaselessly by. A figure appears in a corner, approaches the river, stops before it: only when the figure has stopped can time begin.

It is an element of my torment that this figure must be no other than Gustav. Time can begin only once he is in the picture. I wish it weren't so, that he were unnecessary—things would be simpler for me then. I wouldn't have to deal with a lunatic, for instance. But things are not to be simple for me.

If I actually make it, no one will know what this journey means.

6/25

A loneliness like this has never come over me before. When I get tired of looking for Gustav, I go to the ship. I stand aboard it as if it were my own, and it is, but I am not its captain. Its captain has gone missing.

It gives me strength that the ship we have built is exactly like a real ship—it *is* a real ship—and it is enormous. There are living quarters for 150 people, and they are all empty. I know because I looked in each one of them for Gustav.

The crew tells me they are nearly finished building the pulley that will haul the ship up and over the mountain. But first, they say, they need more money. There is no more money, I told them. Then we will not finish it, they say.

So that's where it stands tonight: Gustav missing, the pulley abandoned, and me, sitting on the deck of my ship looking out into the trees, where man-sized snakes are coiled. Either they are preparing to strike or they are asleep. Sleep is preparation.

There is also a little jungle cat on the deck with me. Each time she looks at me I sneeze. It is the same effect a lover once had on me. I am uneasy around this animal. She keeps rubbing her head against the sides of my boots. I must not give in to the temptation to remove them.

I am cursed: all of my lovers have names that begin with M. This cat reminds me of the first of them—I'm sure it was she who put the curse on me. There was no end of omens when I was with her. The first night we were together, we went walking by the river that flowed through the city where she was living then. She noticed something drifting on the water—"There, look at that," I remember her saying. It looked like a black bowl with a small mast. Then we saw what it was: a black umbrella, opened up and placed on the water like a nutshell, the handle sticking up in the air—an ominous object of unknown meaning.

It's gotten to be that if I meet a woman with a name that begins with M, I must immediately be on guard against all weaknesses in myself. Otherwise I will fall in love with her, and suffer.

A psychologist—I am ashamed to say I once visited one after a lady friend insisted—told me my situation has to do with the fact—the *biological* fact, he said—that the sound of the letter M is one of the first sounds babies make. Across all languages, this psychologist told me, the word for "mother" has a prominent M sound in it. We call the woman whose body we were once part of by the first sound we are able to press out of our lips. After we have finished screaming at the shock of having been separated from her, we bring our lips together and say her name.

Be that as it may, I suspect all psychologists of onanism: believing in their own lies while doubting the obvious.

Later—
The word *interstitial* comes unbidden to my mind. I feel very uneasy tonight, like I could slip through the spaces between the particles of my being and remain situated there, in a there that is nowhere, while the rest of me goes on being Jurgen, making arrangements, filming films, trying to negotiate with nature in doomed endeavor after doomed endeavor, each of which will be misunderstood by others.

I have decided what the ship's name will be.

Later—

There is something that I have not yet been able to make in any of my films. It is more real than everything I have so far made. I know I will never be able to make it—its reality will always evade me. So long as I am there, it, whatever *it* is, is not. Yet I am able to sense it, and that is torment.

Like a rat that has eaten poison once and lived, it stays inside the walls, canny, where it is warm and protected from me. I hear it but am ever unable to catch it. I am dwelling in its trap, which I myself built. It surrounds me.

The cat sits in my lap, purring. The darkness of night is over.

6/27

Today we were to sail the ship up the river to the site where it will be attached to the pulley. Without Gustav we cannot go. I think about the door but I have not gone back to find it. My realm of encounter is the film. Gustav is my door. When will he come here, where I have already created him? I am in the passive position of the waiting lover. My fatal identity is precisely: *I am the one who waits.*

There is a local story about a girl who is born from the river. You might see her white body flash temptingly near the surface, our guide tells me, but you must not offer her companionship. If you do, she will quickly lure you to the bottom of the river, to become a dolphin.

I must keep the river from my mind if I am to remain focused on the insurmountable quantity of work yet to be done. But the river is always here, we are never far from it—the air is always filled with its stench of swamp and carrion.

Incredible heat squeezes a little water out of hell and this falls on us, we who dwell below hell. I slip farther from understanding why I am here into the dream of being here.

Later—
Tonight Gustav came to me in my hut. For a moment I thought I was being visited by a specter as lunatic as the man he once was. His eyes had that wild jabbing intensity of a man trying to crucify himself by looking alone. But no, it was the man himself, Gustav.

Such a man has no specter other than himself.

Raving in the way that he does when he looks like he's about to burst into the form of a wildly different species, or perhaps heat lightning, he said, I found the opening.

Not having the foggiest idea what this lunatic who has had me tramping through the jungle for days in search of him might be talking about, I politely asked, What opening, you worthless idiot?

The door in the jungle, he said. It turns out the door wasn't the opening.

But what *is* the opening, Gustav? *What* opening?

Over at the brothel, a girl, he said. The most amazing child. A way, a passage . . . He got in his eyes a look of dreamy fixation.

So he had been with a prostitute all the time I'd been looking for him. Not a prostitute, a *child*. I remembered the treatment my father used to give the stallions when they escaped and went on sex-crazed stampedes through the mountains. I went right for his scrotum, meaning to separate it from his body. He squealed and hit the back of my neck with his forehead. Then he bit off the tip of my left ear and spat it on the muddy ground.

I let go of his scrotum. He stumbled back, smiling like a boy.

Jurgen, he said, with a look of serene love, you must come with me to see this girl. She's a *fish*, Jurgen.

A *fish*?

I can't explain.

No, I said, no, no, no. I don't want anything to do with her. I don't want anything to do with the river. We must get money somehow to pay the crew so they'll keep building the pulley, so we can pull Molly over the mountain. If I begin to think about the river, I know the film will be doomed.

Who's Molly? asked Gustav.

I crouched to examine the tip of my ear. It was already teeming with red ants. They were dragging it off to some hole, a gift for their queen.

AT THE CENTER OF THE WASP

I had to go back there to bury him. The fucking ground wouldn't give way. It was rotten, so I would have thought it would be soft.

There wasn't even any cement. Aggregate of hair mixed with mud, slapped on with a shovel, with fallen limes rotten on it. Horses festering on rotting hooves dropped shit upon previous shit. The flies. Nothing moved, but always there'd be a buzz coming from green stases of water. Life rearing up from the bottom in slimy bubbles. Blooms drooping, falling rotten on the ground, becoming the rotten ground. There, on the island, one thing becomes clear: that the earth is made of shit and rot. Shit blooming into being, being, then falling into a pile of shit for the sun to shine to dust. And another, secondary clarity: that we are creatures made to find the blooming shit pretty.

The dust was where people there walked. Paths, not sidewalks. Not along the sides of things, which had no clear centers or boundaries, but through the mixed-up muddle of it all, the chaotic plots of homes and markets and shops, churches and mosques and chickens, holy and mundane gnarled with roads that were compactions of dust, which was dirt that was shit once, flowers too. Every living thing a mongrel of every other, or, as he once put it, A bunch of fucking mutts.

The sun, a machine for turning shit back into the shit it had been. Shit that was once flowers became shit again. The flowers therefore were garish, and held within their centers—the flowers had centers, to attract a kind of wasp—a knowledge of rot that they transmitted as succulent oversweet odor. People sucked in this knowledge through their noses to their brains. Wasps inhabited the centers of this knowledge and wove out of its nectar death-gray nests in every cavity and corner. Every cavity and corner held a shelter for the inhabitants of the center of the knowledge of rot, death, and decay. Tourists said it smelled like ylang-ylang. They said it smelled expensive. He sold them this knowledge that it was expensive, what they smelled, the smell of rot, in small bottles they brought in tissued boxes back to states where they held mortgages, jobs. This was the progress of knowledge in a global economy of income inequality, he claimed. What he was selling them was a weapon, and his death interfered not at all with the process. Postmortem, his racket went on from a small shop made of hardened shit in one of the corners of chaos behind an abandoned pomade factory, one of the better neighborhoods of the island.

The island was a turd floating in the murk. It was fecund. He joked that he was a wasp, exactly like a wasp, living in his gray corner of a world built on death, dealing in the profuse knowledge of such yet claiming it to be anything but. Claiming it to be fertile, life-giving, romantic, friendly. Claiming it brought love, success, and admiration to all who dabbed it on their temples. The Western obsession with the temples, he said, the mind, all that. Lots of psychiatrists, he said, visited the island during their wintertime. Do you know what a great chasm of death the ocean is? Yet they fly across it to lie on the edge of it naked. They were youth itself in their feeble, trusting senescence. He would price the little bottles of scent as high as could be maintained by the wasps, the flowers, the shit, the flies, the horses, the sun all working in disordered tandem to make him a little bit rich. A system, he said. I am a system, he said, at the center of the wasp.

A fucking pollinator, he other times called himself, which a wasp was not. I got tired of listening to him—living with him was enough—and walked on the paths of compact shit, admiring the horses' stillness, the steam rising in blasts from former blasts, hot air emitting more hot air, horses no longer horses but gaseous clouds surrounded by unmoving billows of meat-eating flies feasting on each other's wings. The original horse effaced by the cloud of rot that would come to envelope and feed on it. I saw myself in this microcosm of rot, I took the position of the horse no longer horse but a breeding feast of decay. A horse could become any number of flowers people would pick and admire before the rot got them too, though they never admired the rot—and in this, he said, they were misguided to his advantage, because in his scents he put a preservative that went against the whole progress of the place, the movement from rot to rot. My scents never change, he said. Unearth a corpse wearing them and you'll find the scent is the same, even as the flesh decays. You can never kill me (him saying this) because death is how I live.

Well, he died, and the fucking ground wouldn't give. It didn't know what an inch was. But eventually I got a grave shape dragged out of it that I put him in. On the island you're not supposed to bury the dead, because the ground isn't deep enough to keep them from roaming to other lands. But the ground was already made of the dead and decayed, so I didn't see what the difference would be. Also, since he had thought of himself as his scents, especially in his late years, and they were preserved so that nothing of nature could change them, I thought he should be added back to the process, let him decay beneath the flowers that had made him wealthy, let him become the stuff he liked to say he already was. See if his corpse altered the process. See if anybody could detect the dead creator in his scent. Dab him on your temples, wear him out to dinner, let them say you smell exotic (how easily "toxic" becomes "exotic"!). See what kind of future he attracts. I had no plan to keep the business going, but he had left it with someone who understood what he'd meant, I think, by "system."

The little hollow I tucked him in was by the old pomade factory. The once-factory was inhabited by feral cats that had patches missing from their faces. They hissed at me, then ate from my hand whatever I offered them—bread from the market, some bits of fish. Certain ones seemed more like people than other ones. These I probably fed better, though I don't in general regard people highly.

Yet there's a certain bias. For instance, why was I there, digging a hole in an island made of shit? Because of blood.

Because I shared a little of his, and was therefore part of his system. And before all of that I guess I was part of him—him plus a woman, though he always said she was dead.

STORY

I wanted to write the white-tiled entrance to a building. Inside, someone would be waiting for me. I would speak urgently. With thin, glancing enhancements, I would become someone else.

Outside, a yellow flower would be showing. The back end of a car would also be visible.

A bit of red sauce would still be clinging to a yell.

Everything would have meaning in relation to itself. Everything would be a god (another yell).

If this leads to an embankment where I, no longer someone else, am still standing (the car has departed, the yellow flower no longer shows—)

but I don't really have a choice but to keep going. And to go.

I wanted to/somebody else. So I put the yellow flower in a past.

Now it extends effortlessly from a point behind the visible. It permits sight to enter it and disappear. I might wonder about it, but that doesn't mean I like the way my hair is touching my face.

Here I would just like to add a final bit of description to myself—to wonder, I don't need a face.

JAY

One night at a dinner party, our host said that of everyone at the table, Jay was the most likely to be a secret CIA operative or an undercover spy. We laughed out of amusement, then became nervous but kept laughing to cover up what now seemed an eerie possibility: Jay was living a double life. He came to our homes and shared our meals, but he always maintained a distance that let him see us more completely than we could ever see ourselves. After dessert and liqueurs I searched for Jay because I wanted to say goodbye to him before I went home. "Jay?" our host said. "He left an hour ago, you didn't notice?"

For a while I was house-sitting in a wealthy neighborhood. I started to notice something about the trees: many had electrical cords snaking up their trunks. I would see these cords and wonder about them, but it was some time before I thought to look up. When I finally did, I saw surveillance cameras among the branches. "People are avid about watching birds in this neighborhood," I mentioned at the time to a friend. I remember now that that friend was Jay. He never made me feel like a fool, even when I acted like one.

His name was not really Jay. That is just what I am calling him. Since he disappeared, I haven't felt comfortable using his real name. It may be a superstition I am developing—when someone vanishes, they take their name with them, along with our certainty that we ever really knew them. I would not be surprised if, during all of the years of our friendship, Jay was using an alias—not in order to be deceptive, but to protect something, or someone.

I think it is so easy for me to imagine Jay as a spy because he had the most dignity of anyone I have known. The source of his dignity was his patience, which allowed him to be unrelentingly observant. Once, he and I were sitting on a curb in a parking lot of a supermarket, watching the traffic for someone who was supposed to meet us there. While we waited, Jay told me about a test that is given by MI5, Britain's intelligence agency, to people who want to become spies. They are shown a long video of a busy urban intersection. After they've watched the video, they are asked questions, like, How many white cars were in the right lane? How many in the left? In which direction was the cyclist traveling? After about how many minutes did a bird enter the scene? Where did the bird land?

I would not be good at that test—I can't watch a dull scene for more than a minute without my mind wandering far away from it to some trouble I am having in a relationship or to some list of tasks to accomplish. If something seems familiar to me, then it's as if it has already happened, like it's a dream or a memory I'm recalling. Therefore I think I know what's going to happen next, because I've already seen it all. It's a drastic assumption I make out of a kind of laziness.

Jay never would have assumed he knew what was going

to happen next. He would have been great at the spy test. Whenever I was with him he never became distracted, because he never seemed to find any place familiar. It was as if the world and his imagination occupied the same plane, so that to wander one was to wander the other, and to become lost in one was to find himself in the other. He was always attentive to me and our surroundings, aware of the people around us, of our position with respect to all other possible positions, and at the same time he would be listening intently to what I was saying, to the tone with which I was saying it, an apt or clever response always ready. Nothing was happenstance; he could maintain a state of alert-yet-relaxed expectation indefinitely, as if he had never not known a moment in which something startling and unexpected could happen. If he ever *did* become distracted, I never noticed, which I think is the mark of a good spy: he could pay close attention to so many details at once, even if he lost track of one, he still knew exactly what was going on, because the lost one had left its trace among the others.

He once told me something he had observed about human attention. It was during the time, a few years ago, when he was practicing magic tricks—he had thought it would be fun to hire himself out occasionally for entertainment at birthday parties and corporate events. He told me that the eye will follow an object moving in an arc without looking back to its point of origin, but that when an object is moving in a straight line, the eye tends to return to the point where the movement began, the viewer's attention snapping back as if it were a rubber band. As a magician this observation was useful to him, he said, because if he pulled his hand away in an arc at the crucial moment of a trick, the observer would not notice that hand at all, how it tucked the coin under Jay's arm, which was the critical move in that trick if it was to succeed in making the observer believe the coin had vanished.

Jay told me that the key to performing magic was to arrange things so that the observer unknowingly allowed herself to be deceived. The observer had to believe she was being perceptive: that she was seeing all she needed to see, that she knew what she wasn't seeing. The observer's ignorance gave Jay a place to hide.

There was a particular trick that required he have undetected access to the observer's back pockets. He once demonstrated the trick for me. "If I come at you head-on, like this," he told me, stepping forward, "I'm going to run into your personal space very quickly, and that's going to make you uncomfortable." He took a step back. "So, what I do is I give you a point of focus, say a coin. Then I break eye contact by looking down, and I pivot around the point of focus, stepping forward in an arc, or a semicircle, until I'm in your space." He demonstrated, winding up shoulder to shoulder with me, looking up at me sideways. "See how I was able to close the gap?" he said. "Now I have access to all of your pockets."

By the time I became aware of his hand on my back pocket, he had already taken my license and cash from my billfold and placed the billfold back into my pocket. When I later realized what was missing, I called Jay. He asked kindly, "Did you look in your other pocket?"

+

In the week or so before he disappeared, Jay started sending me messages. Of course, when I began receiving the messages, I did not know that Jay would soon be gone. I only thought it was a little strange. We had kept in touch over the years of our friendship, but never this frequently. Now I was getting messages from him nearly every day. In the first message, he wrote, "Today for the first time I understood what a laminate is. It is a picture of wood. For four years I have been walking around on a picture of wood. Not *pictures*, but a single picture, repeated. The grain of the wood in the picture is repeated every three feet (I measured)." That was all he wrote; he didn't sign his name.

I could have written back to him asking him to explain, but I wanted to think about it first. I looked up the definition of the word *laminate*, because even though Jay's message ostensibly explained it, and even though I had never known Jay to be wrong about the definition of a word, I wanted to corroborate what he had written, because what he had written seemed so strange to me. Seeing *laminate* in the dictionary made Jay's message seem less strange.

But when I imagined Jay measuring the pattern—kneeling on the laminate surface of the floor, stretching the tape measure three feet between points he'd determined to be the pattern's beginning—I again felt the strangeness of his message. I thought of him alone in his tower—alone, because he lived alone, and in a tower, because his apartment was a small studio in a cupola beneath a widow's walk. I remember Jay was excited to have found this apartment. He told me it gave him an excellent view of the city's seasons because he could see so many of its trees. Although his apartment was far from the ocean, he said that on windy days, when he looked out over the tops of the trees, he would see them rising and falling in waves, and he could imagine that if he were to leap out into them, he would be surrounded by fish as he drowned.

I decided I would write back asking him whether he was alright. But before I had time to reply, his next message arrived. A ghost shift, Jay explains, is the shift that comes into the factory once it's closed for the night and that manufactures even more of the product off the books. Sometimes the company knows about the ghost shifts and sells its equipment to someone else to make a related but different product than the one the company is making. Or it may be the same product the factory is licensed to produce, but with cheaper materials. But sometimes, Jay continues, the ghost shift happens secretly, among the factory's workers. They use the factory's equipment and only broken, cast-off pieces of the product the factory makes by day, so that the raw materials don't appear to be depleted. They sell these "Frankenstein" (the quotes are Jay's) products on the black market to supplement their meager incomes.

Then Jay writes, "According to a monk I have been reading, each person will encounter in their life one object that is that person's soul. You never know for sure which object is the one, so you have to be careful with everything you touch, and everything you see, both when you are awake and when you are asleep."

I read this message many times. I would get to "asleep" and then start over from the beginning. I found it very unsettling, partly because of the proximity of the words "ghost shift" and "soul"—the proximities of certain words are often unsettling, if they are allowed to persist in the mind—and also because Jay had used the word "soul" at all.

Jay never used a word accidentally. I know that from years of talking and corresponding with him. He had strong ideas about language, about the power of words to create and shape reality, and to make unreal things real. He once told me, during the time when he was working as a magician, that a grimoire—a book of magic spells, a kind of textbook of magic that includes instructions on how to create magical objects, perform spells, and summon supernatural figures such as angels and demons—is nothing more than a grammar, a guide describing how to properly write and speak a language.

After I got Jay's message about ghost shifts and how any object could be my soul, I started looking at the things around me with a new kind of attention. I would look up from my desk and see the sugar maple outside my office window, and I would think, *Maybe that is my soul.* Then I would notice the rocks around it, and the other trees, and the pane of glass through which I was seeing it all, and I would think that any one of these things could be my soul. I was cleaning up a towel I had put beneath the refrigerator to stop a leak from spreading, and I thought, about the towel, which was mildewed and dank, *This could be my soul.* Then I felt a little less disgust with it, and carefully washed it and put it away.

When I put a fresh towel down, both the towel and the pool of water it would soon absorb seemed promising. I even felt it about a paper cut I acquired on my thumb. The little flap of skin kept catching on things and causing me pain, which was something my soul would definitely do, I decided.

A plastic toy car one of the neighbor kids had left on the sidewalk outside my door, the trash the street is always circulating, the perfectly good shirt I never wear because I have seen it so many times—each thing I saw was imbued with the energy of my own body, as if everything was being kept alive by my heart. I especially liked to see the branches of the sugar maple moving in the wind, the hem (in a dream) of a woman's blue dress lapping at her calves as she walked in front of me across a beach, the look on a stranger's face (in the subway) when she saw a good friend she hadn't been expecting to see.

Each movement of my body began to seem like something separate from me, with its own edges I could step into or out of. Each one was possibly my soul.

While walking one afternoon I noticed that a small green pebble was signaling to me. I picked it up and put it in my pocket. It seemed to make my body lighter than it had been previously, so that I floated just a little above the pebbles on the ground.

After a few days, though, the magic began to fade. I no longer looked at the plastic car and thought it could be my soul. The pebble fell out of my pocket one morning while I was putting on my pants. I looked at it on the floor and couldn't figure out what it was, where it had come from. When I remembered, I felt embarrassed. A pebble? I put it in the kitchen garbage, with orange rinds and tissues and coffee filters and other detritus I don't hesitate to throw away. I could have put the pebble outside, but I didn't want to embarrass myself any more. Someone might see me and think I believed in elves and fairies. The kid who had left his toy car might ask me to play. I missed the days when I had believed in the possibility of objects. When, walking in familiar places, I would have the feeling I sometimes get in unfamiliar cities, when doorways and alleys attract me irresistibly, and I feel there is, waiting for me somewhere I am about to discover, a space separate from my life where I will be renewed, restored to an original condition that I never had to begin with. But as the magic of Jay's message began to fade, the possibility of ever finding such a place seemed once again unlikely, a tourist's fantasy. The world went back to seeming mundane.

Then another message from Jay arrived.

I had just come back to my apartment after being away most of the day. I had had a difficult meeting with someone I hadn't wanted to see. I had become so tense by the time I got on the bus home, I felt myself holding on tightly to all of my organs, as if by relaxing I would be allowing them to escape. I had a bad cramp in my stomach as I walked from the bus to my apartment.

I turned the key in the door and stepped into darkness. Immediately I had the sense that someone else was there, or had just been there. The apartment did not feel empty but open, like a passageway connecting two vast, hidden spaces. I told myself that I was tired, and that I could not let myself be persuaded not to enter my own home just because my exhausted mind was anxious.

I went into the living room. There was a narrow yellow shape on the carpet. For some reason I recognized it right away as a message from Jay. I sat on the futon and watched it.

It was coming in through the gap in the curtains. I knew its shape depended on the curtains, and outside the window, on the shifting of the maple's leaves, but no meaning was created by this dependence. The shape seemed completely independent of the tree and the curtain and even of the light it was made of. It seemed like a different kind of object than the ones creating it.

Slowly the message faded. Then the room was completely dark, and I could not see my hands or arms. Usually at night a light outside my apartment turns on intermittently, but some nights it does not turn on at all. When I wanted to get out of the room I had to creep along a wall toward where I knew the light switch was.

Later, in the dark, I lay awake with my eyes closed. Parts of my body would feel far away, like my blood would have to go a great distance in the darkness to reach my head, my hands, my feet. Then all of me would feel close together, and the distance my blood had to travel was not so great. I could have opened my eyes and seen in a glance my body's entire span, but I didn't—I kept my eyes closed, letting myself drift, and after a long time (maybe it was not so long), the bones of my face became heavy, and I fell asleep.

The next morning I woke up feeling unusually good, like after a long illness. When I opened my inbox there was a new message from Jay. "'Once Zhuangzi dreamt he was a butterfly, a butterfly flitting and fluttering around, happy with himself and doing as he pleased. He didn't know he was Zhuangzi. Suddenly he woke up and there he was, solid and unmistakable Zhuangzi. But he didn't know if he was Zhuangzi who had dreamt he was a butterfly, or a butterfly dreaming he was Zhuangzi. Between Zhuangzi and a butterfly there must be some distinction! This is called the Transformation of Things.' The distinction between reality and dreams."

I decided to take the bus to Jay's apartment.

Jay never had people over. He always came to us, to our homes or the bar or restaurant where we were gathered. I had never been to his apartment, though I had his address—he had sent me various parcels over the years, and the return address was always the same. I'd written it down once, thinking I might need it someday.

I found the address, looked up a bus route, drank a cup of coffee and headed to Jay's. I didn't tell him I was coming—his message felt impossible to reply to.

+

When I got to the address I had written down, I was relieved to see, on top of a very baroque (ugly, I thought) Queen Anne house, a cupola and widow's walk.

The house had been divided up into apartments. I followed a path to the side of the house, then started up the stairs leading to Jay's door. I imagined knocking, then seeing Jay's look of surprise, then being invited in for coffee. Jay and I would laugh about the game he was playing with his messages.

But it didn't happen the way I had imagined. I did knock on Jay's door, but he didn't answer. Nobody did. I knocked for a while. After a few minutes, a woman appeared at the bottom of the stairs and called up to me, "He doesn't live here anymore. Moved out yesterday."

I went down the stairs. She said that she lived in the apartment below, and that all day the day before, she had heard a lot of noise coming from Jay's apartment, furniture being moved and things being dropped, and had seen him carrying boxes down the stairs. Where was he carrying the boxes to? I asked her. She didn't know. She said she assumed there was a moving van parked on the street, but from her apartment she can't see much of the street. She said she didn't feel she knew Jay well enough to go outside and ask him what he was up to.

"I was a little intimidated by him, actually," she said. "He always seemed so . . . serious, or something. He seemed like he was apart from everything."

I had never thought of Jay as intimidating, but then, it can be hard to see one's friends the way other people see them. But her description of him as seeming "apart from everything" rang true—even among friends, Jay kept himself a little separate.

About what time yesterday, I asked her, do you think he left?

She said she couldn't say for sure, because she had gone out at seven and wasn't home until after midnight. "Everything was quiet when I got home," she said, "so I figured he was gone."

I thanked her, then sat for a while on the stairs to Jay's apartment, wondering what to do. I looked at the people who walked by on the sidewalk, I looked at the cars that drove by in the street. I even looked at the birds and squirrels. None of it seemed to hold any promise of revealing Jay to me. After a while it occurred to me that I should have asked Jay's neighbor for their landlord's phone number. Maybe Jay had mentioned where he was going. I doubted that he would have, though—I never knew Jay to be forthcoming about his activities.

I felt something enter my body through the metal grating of the stairs: pain. I could not sit on the stairs any longer.

I knocked on the neighbor's door. While I waited I looked at a terracotta pot on the landing that had dry soil and the stalk of a dead plant in it. It was the end of summer. I didn't have a good feeling about anything. I wished I had eaten breakfast. I knocked again, and after waiting a little while longer with the dead plant, I walked to the bus stop and rode the bus back to my apartment.

+

Later that day, I called some friends and asked if they had heard from Jay recently. No, they all said, not a word. Did they know he had moved? No, nobody knew a thing. They were as surprised as I had been to find out. Jay loved that apartment, they all said, why would he leave? I replied to the last message Jay sent me, about Zhuangzi's dream. *Where are you?* I wrote.

Recently one of our friends asked me if I think Jay is still alive. Of course, I said, although sometimes, especially now as the days are getting short and the air cold, I feel uncertain. Still, there are times—early in the morning and late at night—when Jay feels alive to me, and as if he is nearby, hidden among the obvious. I feel this while I'm out walking before breakfast and while I'm lying in bed at night. I listen to a distant train and the cool night air touches my forehead.

Outside my window the leaves of the sugar maple are red and shining. I am impressed by how vivid they become when they are dying. Sometimes I stand at the window, waiting to see one detach and trace the shifting air as it drops to the ground. When I do see one, I feel as if it has fallen just for me.

THE SLOW MAN

There weren't many things to talk about with the slow man. Since he went through the world at such a slow pace, he did not travel far or see many different things. Yet what he did see he would talk about in great detail. He once told her for over an hour about the pattern in the grain of a wood floor. He also spoke to her about nuances he'd noticed in the light and temperature of the few blocks' walk from his apartment to hers. Also, the trees—he would recite their names and tell her many details about them that she would soon forget.

He would call her. When she answered, she would hear a long silence. Eventually, he would say hello.

When he entered her apartment, the thin needles that fell from his body she recognized from when she was a child and would lie beneath a tall pine that sighed as she breathed, that swayed as she waited for something she hoped to be able, one day, to name.

He used an operating system that displayed no images, only line after line of text, which he patiently parsed. He moved through his day in one long, sustained glide, like a silkworm secreting its cocoon.

She did not mind how slowly he moved, though she moved

rapidly, often unable to do one thing for more than a minute before an even greater urgency appeared and needed her to stop what she was doing and attend to it. Because she moved so rapidly, beginning as soon as she woke up and going until long after dark, her health declined—a tremor developed in her right hand, and her left eye spasmed.

When the slow man finally touched her right wrist, she felt a wave of anguish, a slow-motion swan dive that abandoned itself to the gravity of her body. The slow man helped her to walk across the tall, seemingly grass-high carpet to her bed, into which she sank like a melody remembering its beginning.

She very much enjoyed sex with the slow man. He took so long to come! And he made the softest, slowest movements with his cock. Even with his cock, he was never in a rush. Very relaxed, without any tension in their backs or necks, they had sex. Sometimes she had as many as three orgasms, each one creating a wider, more vibratory space in her, before he had even had one.

Her pace began to slow. Even when she wasn't with the slow man, she noticed that she did not go from room to room quite so rapidly anymore. Things did not seem so urgent. She could eat a sandwich before beginning the next task on her dwindling list. Soon, she did not even make a list—there were so few things to do, and she felt she had plenty of time in which to do them.

People who knew her began telling her that she looked younger. *Your skin is so smooth, your hair is so shiny, your muscles are so toned:* they said this about the slow man and also, now, to her.

She and the slow man were getting older, only very slowly. Still, she knew the day would come when they would be subsumed by their surroundings.

She tried more than ever to pay careful attention to the details of what they were becoming—the pattern in the grain of a wood floor, nuances in light and temperature, trees. She looked at the shapes of the leaves, their veins. She remembered all their names.

RICO

A violent coup that had been preparing itself for months was finally happening, he fondly recalls; there was a window in his apartment, and a way of leaning out of it that was like a light shining onto itself. The sound of the cathedral's bell was always imminent in those green moments; a photo of a woman's decapitation by masked men was printed by the resistance, and there was more violence than the humid air could absorb. He would lean from the window to see the courtyard on the rooftop below, where roses tended by a blind man loomed.

Who was the blind man a symbol of back then? The streets had been renamed, but everyone went on using the old names even though to do so, they'd been warned, showed subservience to the previous regime. Something flowering made the air buzz and dream. In the distance, the mountain where he and the wealthy skied.

He remembers the young man, what had his name been, who would enter his room—really he had been a boy—carrying a plate of sliced oranges and almonds the color of skin, the boy's, and the boy had been named Ricardo, Rico, back then.

There was a key hidden beneath a brick; such ways of moving in that dark apartment; such pleasurable, unendurable movements the odor of roses, the shapes of Rico's teeth, the skeletal cathedral's bell, the white chutes of speed he and Rico could achieve. He remembers trying to take an almond from Rico's mouth with his own, and the transition of the almond's smooth peak from Rico's lips to his had been followed by a pleasure so intense—people were protesting in the renamed streets, there were many murders and arrests, on the mountain an avalanche and many deaths—he still makes a sound like a dove when he thinks of it. How when a gun fired, a vein in Rico leaped.

CHOO & CREAM

Around Choo and Cream, or somewhere between their bodies, hung a nearly transparent child who clapped its hands not out of glee or approval, but because of the awkward way its body was hanging, its hands dangling and getting caught sometimes on various cavities of the gaping boots of Choo and Cream.

Clapping, the child often accompanied Choo and Cream when the two did their food shopping. They loved picking over packages of meat for flesh that felt heavier than the weight printed on labels. Yet the child refused to eat the steaks they weighed, so Choo and Cream decided that the child should eat nothing.

But the child was still possessed of energy, like a purse full of money or stolen rings.

The thin, practically lame child felt alive and dangerous to Choo and Cream, and was therefore a liability, as if at any moment the child might scream its own name at passersby, forcing them to hear its terrible voice in places domesticated for purposes of quiet consumption.

Such places were there to police, and the police were Choo and Cream.

The child had appeared one day around the waist of Cream, its face agape with need. The child's face had not been clean.

In a nearby box, a rotating blade distributed hot air around the child's face. Its eyes and mouth did not seem to matter much at all, Cream thought. Choo thought of a ladder of impressive length. Climbing the ladder, Choo imagined never looking down to see Cream and the child disappearing, too small to ever be seen again.

+

Pursuing a speeding driver, Choo and Cream stomped and kicked, trying to push off from their bodies into a leap past speed. There was space for the child in the front seat of the cruiser, but usually, pushed or forgotten, the child slipped down, wrapping around the thick lower extremes of Choo and Cream.

Yet, just as they were about to leave their bodies—to do something drastic to the speeding driver—they felt the weight of the child around their feet, holding them to mere speed.

+

The child was allowed to drink the bean milk Choo and Cream purchased from the discount grocery. This made Choo and Cream feel generous and aloof, for even to go into the discount grocery meant smelling the gluey, wrinkled fruits that grew in lascivious wetness and disgrace. Who were these people? What did their nosy languages mean? Choo and Cream hated to go into the place, but the bean milk there was cheapest, and the people who sold it, apparently cowed by Choo and Cream's matching blue jumpsuits and black boots, did not even look at the child's freakish gait.

It's like these stupid people can't even mate, thought Choo and Cream simultaneously, and winked at the shopkeeper's daughter, or was she the wife? Choo and Cream laughed—it was so much fun not knowing. Here it didn't matter which she was; here she was both.

Choo and Cream always left the discount grocery feeling beyond reproach, with several gallons of the cheapest bean milk. To watch the child drink it disgusted them.

+

It wasn't the child's neck, but some other stickiness that held Choo and Cream together initially. At first, being together had been a form of rest: each had to think less, though there was more to see. What interested Choo came to interest Cream, and what Cream liked to see, Choo had to see, too, and soon there were so many places to be, and so many priorities.

When Choo joined the local fighting committee, Cream joined simultaneously.

As fighters, Choo and Cream moved like different views of the same fist. There were always many things to be fighting, especially the immense ledge jutting from the mountain far beyond town. Since it was predicted that one day the ledge would fall, nothing had been built beneath it. Yet time passed the ledge intact from one day to the next, and the ledge was resented, thought haughty and manipulative. The ledge had human aspects to it—especially at sunset, when it was lit from behind—such as how it sagged almost into the shape of a face, but an ugly one, making it easier to target, hitting it less of a regret.

The ledge—the child looked like it. Wrapping around Cream in a strangulation dream, the child was pure fear at first, and very difficult to eradicate chemically, though Cream tried drinking many things of strong and difficult potencies.

But the child's neck was so strong; its snaky shape insisted on growing something resembling a head, then arms and legs began dangling from Cream, which Cream found so embarrassing since the arms soon had hands that grabbed from between Cream's legs at things Cream didn't even want or need. The child was a thief! At night the child would fall asleep suckling Cream's body, which Choo no longer wanted to touch, yet with the child lying between them, connecting them, Choo had to feel so much.

+

Out in the yard, the child was holding a nostril to the end of the hose, gulping at the dark airlessness of outer space, which the child had seen in a movie about toys. But none of the toys had been able to see what was really happening: nothing. Nothing was happening, and this nothingness was immense—far larger than the boy who sometimes played with the toys by pushing them to the fence, but never beyond the fence. The child hated the fence. The child could see that really everything was drowning in the sky. Nothing, not even the cloud that crossed the child's eyes, could keep anybody alive.

Gulping at what stars were lost in, the child tried to keep its clothes dry so that Choo and Cream would not be disappointed to find that the child had died.

But Choo came too soon to the rescue: Choo came to grill a steak and found the child pooled in a dark fold of its wet clothes, water dripping from its otherwise runny nose.

+

One night, wanting to watch the child sleep, Cream opened the closet where the child's mat was kept.

Sprawled on its mat, the child was disastrous. Its eyes couldn't even be kept shut. They moved around by Cream's feet like the bellies of two dead fish, bumping and lazily deflecting each other.

They are useless to each other and to me, thought Cream.

+

But wasn't there, between its eyes, a little pocket where the child could hide? The child could feel it—a warm border between seeing and the memory of a thing seen: a place between the upholsteries of Choo and Cream into which the child was slipping—and could almost breathe. The child could almost leave its body through a sneeze.

+

The child was playing a game: it was lying on its face, refusing to move from its mat. I hope you decide to go soon, Choo said. Already Choo and Cream were late to make the arrest, but finally they did it: Cream put on the cuffs and Choo carried the child into the cruiser. Immediately the child lay its face against the seat and played at being unable to live.

Through the windshield Choo looked at how small the child really was, how small and distressingly easy to see.

SINCE THE CATS ALL VANISHED

Earth is such a strange planet, riddled with volcanoes and our mistakes. We who live here rarely know our own motives until much too late, after our actions have had time to acquire a dire direction and shape.

For instance, all of the cats vanished in one day. After, we wondered: *When did the vanishing begin?* It was so well coordinated, it had to have been planned. For so many bodies to mobilize, all at the same time, but slyly, without drawing our immediate attention . . . We knew it was no accident, no mistake.

I should pause. I have a tendency to frame my own experience as the experience of a vague and fictional "we." But in this case, it wasn't just Bessie that went missing—all the cats did, not just my beloved calico. And I wasn't the only one wondering how their vanishing was so well planned, and where they all had gone—*we* were all wondering. That they were gone, and so suddenly, spooked everybody.

We agreed that going off somewhere together didn't seem like cats at all. Cats rarely banded together to accomplish shared goals—that was one of the things people who adored them adored about them. They tended, especially as adults, to slink around alone. Even Bessie, who was lethargic and not so ambulatory, liked to explore lofty perches where she could peer out at the world, looking down upon all (except the birds, who watched her warily from higher branches). Sometimes in a dark corner I would see two glowing eyes, watching me so carefully. . . .

Was she planning, even then? Were her withdrawals into dark corners actually tactical maneuvers, mock disappearance-day scenarios?

Because there just isn't enough space on Earth for all of the cats to have suddenly gone off alone, all, it seems, vanishing within the same hour of the same day, I developed an alien abduction hypothesis. There were lots of these floating around, as it turned out. People tweeting and posting about how cats all along were visitors from another planet. On January 21, the day they went missing, their mothership must have come for them.

My alien abduction scenario was followed by other ideas. One was based on something a friend told me about the beetles vanishing for a year after the big earthquake and Fukushima meltdown in Japan. In telling me about the beetles, my friend told me about how, before an earthquake, he would notice unusual behavior among cats—they would congregate together in the courtyard of the large apartment complex where he lived. Ordinarily they never banded together like this; usually they hissed at each other and fought over territory. But once in a while they stopped fighting and came together. They would appear to be doing nothing, just sitting and lying together in a group. Then, suddenly, they would disband. He came to know this as a sign that an earthquake was imminent.

My idea was, I admit, kind of half-baked. There wasn't actually much to it, just that cats cooperate more than we might realize, and they are incredibly sensitive, too. Before a storm, before I even knew a storm was coming, Bessie would compulsively tidy the area around her food bowl and litter box. Frances, when he was still around, learned to help her. First they would painstakingly pick up, using their teeth, any food pellets that had fallen out of their bowls and drop them back in. Then they would do the same for pieces of litter. After everything was tidied, they would hide in a box of old sweaters beneath the basement stairs. It was like they were trying to efface themselves, become traceless. I never figured out why. Maybe they were practicing? Maybe storms had something in common with the sign, whatever it was, that eventually told them all to go?

+

My neighbor Del was the first person I talked to after word had started to spread that the cats were missing. That afternoon, as we lay together in my bed, he remembered how, a couple of years ago, humpback whales had started appearing en masse off the coast of South Africa at a time when they should have been—according to what people had observed them do in the past—in waters hundreds of miles north. Nobody understood what they were doing. Humpback whales tend to be solitary and to hunt alone or in smaller packs, Del pointed out. There must be some kind of change, people reasoned, that we haven't realized yet, something different about their prey, or maybe they sense danger we can't see.

Eventually the whales dispersed and followed their old migration routes. The following year they didn't congregate the way they had, to the considerable relief of people. Nobody has yet figured out what the whales were up to.

"We don't really know jack about other animals," Del said. "A bat, for instance—what is it really like to be a bat? There's this essay by a philosopher about how truly weird it must be—utterly beyond human comprehension—to be a winged mammal equipped with a sensory apparatus that lets you see by interpreting sound waves even as you zoom at forty, fifty miles an hour through the darkness catching insects. I mean, when I try to imagine what it's like to be a bat, I end up imagining what it's like to wear a hairy parachute and fall through the air, screaming. Even in my imagination I'm limited by my senses."

Before going to Del's, I'd spent the morning calling for Bessie and searching around the yard where I knew she liked to hide. At some point I remembered the box under the stairs.

The box of my mother's sweaters.

I didn't find Bessie there, but a flap of the box was up, and in the box a blanket of Bessie's hair covered my dead mother's red cashmere sweater, the one she would wear on Christmas Eve and that I hadn't been able to get rid of since her death.

Seeing my missing cat's hair on my dead mother's sweater gave me an eerie feeling, as if the two of them were hanging out in the afterlife together. I thought of something I had read about how, for a time in Egypt, people worshipped a cat goddess, Bastet, who protected all cats and also generally conferred fertility. When a pet cat died, its owner would have it mummified so that its spirit would be able to find its body in the afterlife. In the 1800s, an Egyptian farmer discovered a large tomb filled with, it turned out, eighty thousand mummified kittens and cats.

My thoughts twisting, I wondered, *Was Bessie drawn to this box because it belonged to a dead person?*

No, I decided, more likely this sweater comforted Bessie not because it had belonged to my mother, or to a dead human, but because the soft furry fabric reminded Bessie of *her* mother. Somehow among all the boxes, Bessie had found the one containing a mother-remnant, and she would return to it when she was anxious.

Maybe something like this was happening right now, I thought, only on a grand scale, affecting all of the cats—a vast mother-remnant had been found, and its location communicated among the cats by means of a cat language that had eluded humans. When their anxiety peaked, the cats all knew where to go.

Or maybe Bastet, protector of cats, had become angry, and had vanished the cats as retribution? Maybe Bastet's next move would be to make us all sterile.

I went upstairs, sat at my desk. I typed "do cats" and was offered the following suggestions to complete my search:

"Do cats prefer to die alone"

"Do cats go away for days"

"Where do cats go when they die"

"Why do cats hide when they are sick"

I searched "Do cats prefer to die alone."

None of the results seemed promising—discussions on forums, some devoted to amassing evidence of psychic connections between cats and their owners. But one thing did catch my eye: at the bottom of the first page, a link to a related search: "Where did all the cats go."

I clicked on it. More links to forums, including one I read occasionally. I followed that link into a discussion presently unfolding among people whose cats were missing.

"I've heard cats like to go off alone when they are dying," posted somebody named MrMC. "But Mr. Biggs was three years old. He was healthy. I don't think he was dying. He has never been away from home this long in his life."

Hundreds of replies. Other posts echoing MrMC's. Hundreds of replies to each of those. People agreeing: their cat didn't die. Their cat never stayed out the whole night. Their cat was an indoor cat; their cat was afraid of grass. How had the cat even gotten outside? Could the cat be hiding somewhere inside? "I live on the top floor in a 400 sq. ft. apartment, I can see every inch and not one has my cat in it," wrote Exxor090.

The obvious thrust of these discussions was that cats were

missing from places where reason and physical laws of the universe strongly suggested they should still be.

I wasn't sure where this left me. Feeling a little better because I wasn't alone in missing a Bessie; feeling worse because the universe was clearly acting oddly, if not irrationally, by making it possible for so many cats to have simultaneously vanished.

I opened Twitter. #missingcat and #gatodesaparecido were trending. On Facebook three friends had already posted about their cats. For me to post about Bessie seemed redundant, but I did it anyway—maybe my post would add a little weight to the critical mass needed to create news out of a series of related anecdotes.

On Snapchat it was already an "event" that the cats were missing. It was like the election—an audience of millions, all of us shocked to be talking about the same thing.

"Is this really happening? Are all the cats gone?"

"They have to have gone *somewhere*."

"Where do cats go when they disappear?"

"Cats don't disappear."

With this last I agreed—my own experience with cats told me that they don't disappear. Rather they lurk, they hide, they scheme. And then they pounce.

What were the cats up to? Was Bessie about to leap on me?

I swiveled around in my chair.

Nothing was there. Just my office.

I didn't want to be alone in front of a screen anymore. I got up, put on coat and boots, and walked next door to the Ingrams' house. They had two cats, Mimi and Flowers. Sometimes Mimi and Flowers would visit Bessie, and the three of them would sit in the yard, in a sort of lopsided triangle formation, staring at each other. Then, after an amount of time that might have seemed vast to cats or nil—I'm not sure what time felt like to cats—one of them would wander off, and soon the other two would, too.

Del answered my knock. "I wanted this not to be happening," he said when he saw me.

+

Del Ingram and I had been sleeping together for several years. His partner, Julia, was a high-powered lawyer and wouldn't get home until ten, eleven o'clock at night. Often she would be at the office on the weekend. Del works from home; he's a cartoonist. I work from home, too. Soon after I moved in, we started noticing each other because we were both always at home.

I would wave to Del from my yard; he would wave from his. Once in a while he'd call, "How's it going?" I would reply, "Okay. You?"

Del and I became closer after Frances was killed. Not long

after I moved in, a mail carrier, not the usual one, drove a mail truck up the driveway, something the usual carrier never did. Frances was old and slow. The truck crushed his head, yet he still managed to drag himself in through the cat door. He got himself just inside the door before he died. I found his body when I came home. I was devastated. His head and neck were crushed. I thought at first some sicko had murdered him and then, in order to scare me, pushed him in through the cat door. I was in a frenzy. Who would do such a thing? I ran next door, because I'd met the Ingrams and they seemed nice. They'd lived in the neighborhood for years. Maybe they would know if this kind of thing was a regular occurrence, something the realtors never tell you.

Julia was at work, but Del was home and he made me a cup of peppermint tea with honey and sat with me until I calmed down. Together we went back to my house.

We found Bessie crouched beside the corpse. She was licking the wounds. I cried. It was messy. There was blood, plus me in tears, unable to deal with the cleanup. Del looked around and started helping. He got Frances onto an old sheet and wrapped him up like a mummy. He set him on the porch and told me I might consider where I'd like to bury him. He cleaned up the blood in the entryway, mopped the floor. I decided Frances would be buried under the magnolia in the backyard. That was Frances's tree. He liked to perch on one of the lower branches. He would spend hours there, looking down at our yard, looking out at the other yards. Once, I found him napping on that branch, his two front legs dangling down on either side of it. When the tree was in bloom it had big white flowers the color of Frances's fur. It seemed to me Frances knew how good he looked in that tree. Frances was a dandy.

Del dug a hole in the tree's shadow and together we lifted Frances's wrapped corpse into it. Del handed me the shovel and told me I should put the dirt on top of him, so I did, crying. We put a stone on the mound and Del and I stood there for a while. Del put his arms around me in a friendly, consolatory way.

Two days later Del and I were together in my bed.

It was safer at my house. Nobody would come home at an unexpected time, or at any time at all. After Frances died I only had Bessie. Bessie didn't seem to care for Del. When Del was there, Bessie wouldn't come near the bed.

It was her way of tacitly disapproving of me, it seemed. Her silence and absence were much more condemnatory than if she had, say, hissed at Del when he walked in the door. Instead, she would vanish until well after he left.

Now I am wondering whether the cats vanishing is their way of showing people, on a grand scale, how deeply they disapprove of how we are living.

But other cats weren't as good with the cold-shoulder routine as Bessie was. Frances, for instance, would cuddle with anybody, anytime, without regard for whether or not they were committing marital infidelity.

Since the cats vanished, Del comes over more often. When Julia leaves for work early in the morning, he's all alone over there—no Blossom or Mimi. They made working from home less lonely for Del, just as Bessie and Frances had for me. Bessie mostly kept to herself, yet there was still a mutual feeling, even when it seemed she was deliberately being aloof. There was a co-dependence that felt like company, companionship. Bessie always knew more or less where I was. She tracked me, her food source, not exactly as a wild cat might track its prey, but maybe not so unlike that, either. I grew accustomed to the feeling of being tracked. I found it comforting. I liked knowing that another creature knew where I was, even if only because I was the one with the food, the fish-flavored pellets I'd drop in Bessie's bowl twice a day.

If the cats were trying to punish us by disappearing, or teach us a lesson, in some ways it's worked, and in some ways it hasn't. I haven't noticed people living more upright, less wasteful lives. On the other hand, we're lonelier, more afraid than we were before. I think we're all aware now that we're not in charge—this process, *nature* we might call it, has its own shape, its own trajectory. We're part of it, and we're not in control of it at all.

A few mornings ago, while Del and I were lying in my bed, it occurred to me that maybe the cats' reason for leaving hasn't been revealed yet. It's still coming. It's like those cats slinking off before an earthquake. One moment they're all huddled together in the courtyard, and the next they're gone, having sensed something approaching, something about to rip apart the surface of the earth.

Like I told Del the other day: Whatever it is, it must be on its way.

7 TOUCHES OF MUSIC

1

In a day without images, in a night without time, we are going to the Museum. In the Museum the figures stand facing the walls; the halls get longer as we walk them; dust in its purest form is longing.

2

A rose is spinning, spinning without an axis. Its axis is memory.

3

Inside a crow's body, metal sheaths emit hollow gasps and sighs, sometimes little puffs of mist. Is the sea that lies at the bottom of all forgetfulness sucking on the spiny bodies of deep-dwelling crustaceans? Yes, they are the organs of intelligence. The crow transports them by day and by night.

4

A pineapple being whipped in a gray room by a naked man who crouches and leaps, wearing only a leather band around one wrist. This man appears to be covered in glitches; the image he's part of has suffered a loss of identity. It cannot recognize itself and tries to fling little pieces of its body away. The little pieces are shed like dandruff. A symptom of irritation.

5

A knife—a boning knife—being force-fed cotton candy. The torches have been lit even though it is still bright outside. Without anyone, the Ferris wheel spins, flinging off its empty carriages, returning to its origin. Facts are collapsing; the tent of animals gasps, its red walls heaving like annihilation, while the dead ones come.

Daily we adorn ourselves for pageants such as this.

6

Q: Today will the names of things glisten?

A: Yes, and the tongues.

Q: And if the urge of words is to be wrought as objects, will it be done?

A: Nothing will be undone today. The roots are swallowing their beginnings.

Q: Will the rat be back?

A: The rat never left.

Q: And the darkness that saw me slinking?

A: I am the darkness that saw you slinking, and all my eggs have hatched.

7

Escape leaves a heavy streak of silver in the air that crumbles into white dust. It falls on the grass and the silences between

leaves. We walk through a crowd of mists, seeing again and again the same face among the veils. Sometimes in a mirror I notice it looking at me: speech. The animals use us to give their sounds meaning; we attribute to a growl a known sentiment: what's visible to us is an extrusion of what's visible to *them*.

It's not true that dust was once my skin.

—

An unaccounted for music is produced by placing my heart on a heavy stone. This must be done during the dry season, near hives of honeybees, at the time in late afternoon when everything on earth is alone. A small wood box containing yellow must be kept on a dusty shelf; heat will bleed sap from the grain of box and shelf, adhering them. Then, a gentle rustling will be heard in a part of the house we can't see during the dry season, near hives of honeybees, at a time in late afternoon when everything on earth is alone.

AIR

You reach a point and think, *There's no going back from here*, but of course you can always go back, though you may no longer be able to find the place where you started, the place where you began, the place where you were before you thought, *There's no going back from here*, you can still go back, you can still turn tail and head back the way you came, though the way you came may have utterly changed, may have a totally different appearance, may be filled with unfamiliar trees and buildings and faces, and everything may seem strange to you. Or else the place where you started might no longer be intact, it might be a shambles, it might be in pieces on the ground, in ruins, and the ground might be different, too, it might have a totally different aspect than the ground where you started, so that it is unrecognizable as the ground where you started, and the people, who are also a shambles, might look at you differently than they used to look at you, in the place where you began before you began, still, you can always go back, even at the point when you think, *There's no going back from here*, you can always go back, though the way back may be unrecognizable to you, and you unrecognizable to it.

Recently, just recently I wanted to buy a new, larger pot for a plant that had outgrown its current one, the plant is really quite remarkable in its relentless growth, in flourishing unrelentingly, it's all I can do to keep up with it, to obtain for it, on its behalf, all of the water and sunlight and nutrients it needs for its unrelenting growth, but buying the pot kept eluding me. For weeks I kept trying to buy this new, larger pot, I knew exactly what kind and size of pot I needed to buy, yet I could not buy the pot. I would go to buy the pot and something would happen, I would realize mid-way to the store that I had forgotten an important appointment that was starting imminently, even though I never have important appointments, or, once, that I had forgotten my wallet, even though I don't have a wallet, just an envelope where I keep the cards and bills that are for some reason necessary to carry at all times, at all times in public one must be carrying on one's body, in some pouch or pocket affixed to or hung from one's body, by way of clothing or a bag made of another animal's skin, or made to appear to be made of another animal's skin, these cards and bills, otherwise one is useless, one cannot purchase pots or anything at all, so I gave up that day on trying to buy the new, larger pot, and the next time I tried I ended up giving up, too, though I can't recall why, what, if anything, happened to make me decide not to go through with it after all, not to go and buy the new, larger pot I had for weeks been trying to buy, even though the stars seemed aligned, so to speak, everything seemed in order for buying a pot that day, I had my envelope of cards and bills and a clear schedule, still, there was some obstacle, something preventing me, so that once again I did not buy the new, larger pot.

The fact was, at some point I finally had to acknowledge that the fact was, I didn't *want* to go and buy the plant a new, larger pot, even though it needed one, even though each time I saw the plant I would feel a little bit guilty, knowing it needed a new, larger pot, knowing exactly what kind of pot it needed and that I could go and buy this pot if I wanted to, but despite what I knew to be true about the plant and its need for a new, larger pot, I didn't want to go and buy it a new, larger pot. In fact, going out to buy the plant a new, larger pot was the last thing I wanted to do.

What I regret most, what I actually regret the most, is how everything ends up so exaggerated. By some mechanism, between its occurrence and its recollection, between happening and happenstance, each thing ends up exaggerated, warped, distorted, out of proportion, barely the thing it was, barely the thing it used to be, before, when it occurred, before it was recollected, before its scattered pieces were collected in a gross exaggeration of its original form. Buying the plant a new, larger pot wasn't the *last* thing I wanted to do. It was not, of all possible things to do, the ultimate or final thing, or even the penultimate or semi-final thing. There were many other, much more troubling, much more vexing and painful and expensive things that were actually the *last* things I wanted to do, like having my wisdom teeth pulled out or sorting through the pile of supposedly important mail that had been accumulating for months, like detritus on a beach, or like detritus on any plane cyclically engulfed by an enormous entity that is filled with detritus, on the floor beneath my desk, or looking for a new job, to say the least. Buying a new, larger pot for a plant that badly needed a new, larger pot should have been nothing compared with the other difficult things on the agenda, should have been the thing I did first, to be able to cross something easy off my list, to buoy my spirits, so to speak, which were always badly in need of buoying, because they were always sinking, my spirits, they were always in the midst of sinking beneath the detritus, and if not sinking then they were sunken, totally waterlogged and taking on water fast, going down, approaching bottom, approaching the unfathomable abyss, so to speak, so that anything living in them, any life whatsoever dwelling in my spirits, was in imminent danger, at all times, of drowning, of suffocating to death.

Still it seemed to me, whenever I considered enacting it, that buying a new, larger pot was the last thing I wanted to do. The last thing I wanted to do was drive to the plant store, enter the plant store, navigate to the new, larger pot, carry the pot to the counter, strike up another one of those unsatisfying conversations that are meant to mitigate, for both parties, the discomfort of the transaction, then carry the pot to the car, drive home with the pot on the seat beside me, carry the pot into the house, only to face the difficult task of getting my large, unrelentingly vigorous plant out of its old pot, the one it had outgrown, its roots having completely filled its old pot, to the point where they were pressing against the sides of its old pot, threatening at all times to burst from the old pot, to burst forth into the room, something I feared, since this plant, this unrelenting plant, intimidated me with its un-relentingness, its extreme zeal for growing and flourishing, I didn't know what to make of it, how to approach it, except to try to live respectfully alongside it, the way one might try to live in the presence of a world leader or professional athlete or successful entrepreneur, try to give it all it needed for its unrelenting growth while also staying out of its way, not interfering, to maintain a certain distance between us, a distance the pot was an integral part of, the pot was the key to the distance I tried to maintain between myself and the plant, and if the pot were to burst, if the unrelenting plant were to press and press its roots against the sides of the old pot until the old pot finally burst, an outcome the plant may have been trying, in its slow, vegetal way, to achieve, then the distance between us would collapse, there would be nothing between me and this improbable plant that insisted on flourishing relentlessly, despite all odds, which seemed, in my experience, the odds all seemed in my experience to be hostile to life of every sort except perhaps bacteria and jellyfish, bacteria and jellyfish flourish no matter how hostile the conditions, no matter how hot or how acidic or how decrepit, and I had to keep something between us, yet to get the plant into a new, larger pot I would most likely have to break the old pot, if the plant had not already, by the time I arrived home with the new, larger pot, burst from its old pot, then I would have to get a hammer and smash it, the old pot, smash it to pieces, to get the plant out, and then lift the plant, this insuperable creature that is taller than I am, into the new, larger pot, making sure to cover its roots with new, fresh soil, which would also have to be purchased from the plant shop, and more than anything, I dreaded, in anticipating buying a new, larger pot, forgetting to buy the soil and having, in the midst of my struggle to wrest the plant from its old pot into the new, larger pot, to drive back to the plant shop for the soil, then drive back to my home, making sure to water the new soil once it covered the plant's perpetually thirsty roots, water and water the new soil covering those forever famished roots, until water flowed from the bottom of the new, larger pot onto the floor, collecting there in a puddle, a small, circumscribed abyss, which would then have to be mopped, and once mopped, polished, lest the wood warp or rot, or warp and rot.

Each time I saw the plant, each time I passed the room where the plant was flourishing relentlessly, insuperably, despite the odds, despite its pot being too small, so that I was certain the pot was about to burst, I would think, *It needs a new, larger pot*, and then I would think of what buying a new, larger pot would entail, and I would know, with absolute clarity, with total certainty, a certainty that I experienced with respect to no other area of my life, that yet another day would pass, yet another day would deposit its detritus beneath my desk without my having bought the plant a new, larger pot. I knew it would not be any better, it would not be any easier to buy a new, smaller pot, no, or even an old, larger pot, my dread had nothing to do with the new pot or the qualities of the new pot, but with everything surrounding the new pot: the car I would have to drive to the plant shop; the road to the plant shop; the plant shop; the cashier at the plant shop and the words exchanged; the money I would have to pay to purchase the pot from the plant shop; the car I would then put the pot into, once it had been purchased; the road I would follow home, to my home, where I would have to maneuver the pot out of its old pot and into the new, larger pot, possibly smashing the old pot with a hammer; the hammer; and of course the plant itself, since I wouldn't be in this mess, I wouldn't have to feel guilty each time I looked into the room of my home where the plant was flourishing relentlessly, I wouldn't have to consider the possibility of its bursting forth from its old pot and the distance between us collapsing, so that no distance between me and this relentless, enduringly vigorous plant remained, I wouldn't have to think about any of this if I'd never had the plant to begin with, if the plant, for me, had never existed. Because I *did* have this plant, because the plant, for me, existed, I dreaded everything, the entire world around the plant, everything between me and the new, larger pot, and then everything between me and my home, where I would put the new, larger pot, became dreadful to me each time I saw the plant and thought, *It needs a new, larger pot.*

It was at this point, no sooner and precisely no later, that I decided, I felt I had to resolve, to get rid of the plant, the plant had to be gotten rid of, I decided, in order to rid the world of the dread the plant inspired in me, so that I could walk into that room of my home, the room where the plant was, without wanting to run in the other direction. But it was such a large plant, the plant was so unwieldy, since it had been growing unceasingly, night and day, pulling into itself all of the water and sunlight and nutrients it possibly could, I knew I would not be able to get rid of it all at once, I would have to do it piecemeal, cutting pieces off the plant and carrying the pieces away, outside my home, into the woods, *into the woods*, I heard myself say, but which woods? Which woods did I mean to carry the plant, piece by piece, into? After all, what was I talking about? There was no woods, I knew of no woods anywhere near my home, the nearest woods was miles away, at least seven miles away. Did I, then, intend to drive the plant, piece by piece, to the nearest woods, which was at least seven miles away? Or did I intend to cut up the plant into pieces, then carry all of the pieces, one by one or several by several, to my car, and then drive all of the pieces at once to the woods, which was at least seven miles away, or drive some of the pieces at once, then return for more of the pieces, seven miles at least, and carry the pieces one by one or several by several into the woods? I couldn't believe that that was what I intended, that any of it was what I meant to do, whether one by one or several by several, whether all at once or piece by piece.

And so, incredulous, I did nothing. I waited, truth be told, until I knew what I had really meant, until I knew exactly what I had intended when I had thought those words, *into the woods*.

Soon, a matter of minutes or perhaps hours or days later, I can't recall, I knew, exactly, what I had meant by those words, *into the woods*. I remembered that there was, in fact, a woods near my home, less than half a mile from my home, though it was not the sort of woods just anyone could walk into, since it was surrounded by fences, tall fences with razors along the top, whether to deter or contain was hard to say, since I didn't know what went on in that woods, the fences could have been meant to both deter and contain, to keep something out and to keep something else, something other than the thing kept out, in, I had never figured out what went on in that woods since I had never been allowed to pass through the fences, had always followed the warning that was posted every ten or twelve feet along the fences to KEEP OUT, though I had walked along the edge of the forbidden zone, alongside the fences and the woods the fences kept me out of, many times, many times in the mornings and many times in the evenings, when I was out for a walk I would decide to go to the woods and I would walk alongside the fences surrounding the woods, peering through the fences at the woods within, listening to the chirps and rustlings within, wondering what went on within the woods within the fences, where I wasn't allowed to go and so where I had never been. I remained outside the fences, at all times I never entered them, I followed the warning to KEEP OUT rigorously, never setting one foot inside the fences, never even poking a finger through them, although I looked through them, with my eyes I entered the fences, so in a sense I may be said to have trespassed, I may be said to have violated the warning to KEEP OUT, though looking revealed nothing to me except that here was a woods I was forbidden to enter. Going in there, even knowing what went on in there, if anything, was off-limits to me, so I stayed where I was allowed to be, outside the fences, knowing nothing of why this woods was forbidden to me.

What about woods, what exactly about a *woods*, or exactly what about *this* woods, had to be forbidden? The trees themselves, or what happened among the trees? Maybe I was wrong in thinking that this was a *woods?* Maybe this was something else entirely, the trees merely a curtain, a facade, for the thing the fence was actually surrounding, forbidding me to enter? Maybe only the edges, the perimeter, was woods, and the center, the core, was something else entirely, some sort of structure that had to be shielded from sight? I didn't know what I wanted to see when I looked through the fences, but I wanted to see something. Even though I thought of this place as a woods, seeing trees, seeing a dense growth of trees and among the trees, shadows and darkness, seeing a woods even when I expected to see a woods, wasn't satisfying. I wanted to see, apparently, something else besides trees in this woods. Each time I walked along the fences I looked through the fences, wanting to see something besides what was apparent: trees and the shadows between trees, a woods, in other words, and never anything other than a woods, as far as I could see, which, tantalizingly for me, wasn't very far. Likely I couldn't see any farther than I would be able to throw the pieces of the plant, were I to throw the pieces of the plant, over the fence, since the fence was quite high, it was a tall fence, the pieces of plant wouldn't go far beyond the fence, once they were over the fence, if I could get them over the fence, if I could throw them that high, they would drop down just on the other side, landing with the soft heaviness of recently living matter, among still-living matter, the trees and plants of the woods, which might have been a facade.

Maybe that's why it's forbidden, I thought, otherwise anyone could walk in with any quantity of recently living matter and dump it there, the way I wanted to dump the pieces of plant, just walk right into the woods and dump dead stuff everywhere, and if it wasn't forbidden then the woods would soon be full of dead stuff, engulfed with dead stuff that people had dumped, including the pieces of my plant, which I longed to be rid of.

The woods being forbidden, then, protected the woods, I saw how the woods being forbidden to me protected the woods from me, from me and from people like me, from me and from the thing I could not look at without feeling guilty, without feeling like I wanted to rid the world of this thing, not only the world outside of me but the world within me, my memory, completely rid my memory of this thing I felt guilty seeing, chop it up into pieces and dump it all at once or piece by piece, howsoever, in the woods, which, being forbidden, was protected against just this, against just this sort of tactic of ridding one's world of guilt, and also, incidentally, against the thing gotten rid of, which, who knows, considering how vigorously and relentlessly such guilt-inspiring things often flourish, might find some way of taking root, once dumped in the woods the thing might take root there, and then continue to flourish, relentlessly, with the utmost vigor, taking in as much nutrition as it possibly could, pulling into itself through its aggressive roots as much nutritive matter as possible, and continuing, unceasingly, to grow, to spread itself both aboveground and below, slowly and inexorably spreading itself throughout the air and the ground below.

That is why the fences are so high, I reasoned, to prevent such things from dropping down on the other side, in the woods, and there continuing to grow, there continuing to spread inexorably aboveground and below.

Still, I thought, *how much easier things will be once the plant is out of my home!* Whether it took root in the woods and continued to grow was no concern of mine, because it would be out of my sight and, as they say, out of my mind, most of all I wanted the plant out of my mind, completely gone from my mind, I realized, not just from my home but gone from my mind, in fact it didn't matter to me whether the plant remained in my home, I realized, as long as it was gone from my mind, completely gone. *Why not forbid the plant from entering your mind,* I thought, *the way you are forbidden from entering the woods?* I could see where I was going with this the woods/my mind comparison—build a tall fence, and around it place signs telling all to KEEP OUT. I thought, *Might there not be a way, then, to keep the plant in your home yet completely out of your mind?*

No, of course not! Just as I could peer through the fence at the woods within, the plant would be able to peer through the fence I constructed around my mind at my mind within, or at the woods around my mind within, if it were possible to construct a fence and a woods around a mind, which it wasn't, I knew very well that it wasn't possible, I knew very well that it was impossible to construct a fence and a woods around a mind, since the mind is a transitory phenomenon, a transitorily instantiated epiphenomenon, the only way would be to construct a fence and a woods around myself, my body, and thereby around my mind, yet I could not build fences or a woods, or fences and a woods, around myself, inside of my home, because I needed to be able to move freely in my home, I wanted to be able to go into any room at any time, I did not want to have fences or a woods around me inside of my home, that would be worse, I decided, much worse than having the plant inside of my home.

But if I put a fence around the plant, I wondered, what if I put a fence around the plant? A fence and a woods around the plant? At which point I realized I was more or less back to where I had begun, contemplating the same tactic of cutting the plant into pieces and going to the edge of the woods and throwing the pieces over the fence surrounding the woods into the woods, and having circled back to this tactic I knew it had to be done, had to be realized, finally, as the only way to get the plant out of my mind, completely gone from my mind, the only way to put between my mind and the plant a woods with fences forbidding me from entering the woods was to throw the plant into the woods with fences forbidding me from entering the woods, since to be forbidden from entering a place is the greatest protection for both the place and from oneself, especially when that place contains something one wants gone from one's mind, being forbidden from entering the place where one might encounter the thing one wants gone from one's mind is a great protection, since to encounter the thing one wants gone from one's mind surely reinstates the thing within one's mind, encountering the thing one wants gone from one's mind, completely absent from one's mind, is the surest way to find the thing once again inside of one's mind, instantly within one's mind again, absorbed once again by one's mind.

I began cutting the branches off with a knife, a sharp knife I used in the kitchen to cut up vegetables I intended to cook. As I did this, cutting off the branches with a knife, separating with the blade of my sharpest paring knife the plant's branches one by one from the plant's thick main stalk, I had the sense that I was preparing to cook and then to eat the plant since the knife was the one I used to cut up vegetables I intended to cook and eat, yet here I was using it to cut up, essentially, a vegetable, although not one I intended to cook, and not one I intended to eat, and this created some dissonance in me, using this familiar object, the knife, in an unfamiliar way, to cut up a vegetable I did not intend to cook and certainly did not intend to eat, but that I intended to carry piece by piece, or perhaps all of the pieces at once if I could manage it, to the woods, to the fence forbidding me from entering the woods, and then to throw piece by piece over the fence, into the woods I was forbidden from entering. As I had never before used the knife in this way, I began to see it, the knife, in a new light, so to speak, although of course the light was not new, and it was illuminated by the same old familiar light, the light of the sun, and as the sun declined, the light of the lamp. Yet, as I used this familiar object, my knife, in a new way, in a room where I had never before used it, everything familiar around the knife was changed, including the light in the room, it shone and reflected and appeared in a new way, a way never before seen by my eyes, since never before had I done what I was doing with this knife.

When I pressed the knife into its flesh, the plant excreted a substance, a viscous liquid, undeniably an ooze, from its flesh, as soon as I pressed the blade of the knife into the plant, instantaneously it began to excrete a thick liquid right there around the abscission, around the wound, and I realized I was wounding the plant mortally, since it was my intention to kill the plant, in order to rid my mind of the plant first I had to kill it by cutting it into pieces, branch by branch, and then carry the pieces to the woods and throw them over the fence into the woods, first I had to mortally wound the plant, which oozed from its wounds, something I had not foreseen. (Is it ever possible to foresee an ooze?)

I felt, I began to feel the slightest regret as soon as the plant oozed where I had cut the first branch, I began to feel the slightest regret about my decision to mortally wound the plant and carry it piece by piece to the woods, and as I continued cutting the branches off the plant, and the plant continued to ooze, I felt more and more regret, until, by the time I was cutting off the last branch from the plant's thick main stalk, I was engulfed in regret, swimming, so to speak, in regret. As I looked at the pile of the plant's branches on the floor, its vigorous branches that had put forth so many leaves and flowers, and then at the plant's thick main stalk, which was now bare of branches and leaves, just a vertical stick in a pot, I was so to speak swimming in regret about what I had done, which at this point I could see no way not to have done, to undo, and seeing no way to undo what I had done, I felt it was even more necessary, more important than ever before, to get the plant out of my mind, completely out of my mind, to get the plant into the woods, beyond the fence forbidding me from entering the woods, and thereby out of my mind.

The ooze was sticky. It got on my hands and, when I wiped my hands on them, my pants. *Of course these oozes always get on everything, that is their purpose, to signal distress, the plant's distress, to scream, in a sense, cry out, warn the others, furthermore it is probably poisonous,* I thought. It was a thought of remorse.

So the ooze had worked its purpose. It had cried out, of the plant's distress, and now I had the plant's cry all over my hands and, what was more, all over my pants, I was swimming in it, a viscous manifestation of my regret, I realized, as I went to the kitchen to wash my hands and, truth be told, to regroup, to try to regather myself, as I felt myself to have dissipated, to have been exhausted to the point of vanishing, by what I had done to the plant.

From the kitchen, hands clean, I looked into the room where the plant was. There it was. But it was no longer *the plant,* hardly could it be called *the plant* anymore, now that all of its branches were in a pile on the floor, dripping ooze on the floor, and its main stalk, also dripping ooze, was just a line in a pot, a vertical, relative to the floor, where the branches lay all in a welter, line, indicating, guiding my eyes, it appeared, to the area just beneath the room's ceiling, an area I had given little thought to before, had never deliberately noticed before, this area the plant and I had been living beneath, but now I regarded it attentively, since the plant, what remained of the plant, a vertical line extending from a pot beside a pile of its own branches, seemed to be indicating, to be guiding my eyes to this area precisely, this area of risen, trapped air.

There's no going back from here, I thought. This was the point at which I thought, *There's no going back from here*. Of course there wasn't anything there, there was only a vacancy, the area just beneath the ceiling appeared empty as usual to me, nevertheless I sensed something there, if only because what remained of the plant, a line, appeared to be indicating something there, to be guiding my eyes specifically to this air, to this area of air I had exhaled while cutting off the plant's branches, mortally wounding the plant, the plant, what remained of the plant, this oozing line in a pot, was indicating the air I had breathed during its murder, and the warm, expired air was hovering just beneath the ceiling. I saw it, could not help but see it, this vacancy above me, as a bad omen, a dark cloud on the horizon, a bad sign, both the vacancy and the oozing indication made me hesitate, since even if I were to go ahead and carry the plant's branches and main stalk to the woods, the area of air just beneath the room's ceiling would remain, and there was no way, I could think of no way, to rid the room of the area just beneath its ceiling, though maybe I could rid the area of its air, rid the area just beneath the ceiling of the trapped, expired air, its suffocating air trapped beneath the ceiling. Maybe by opening a window, by opening all of the windows in the room, as soon as I was back from throwing the plant's pieces, and also the plant's old pot—I realized the pot would have to go, too, if the plant was to be gone from my mind—over the fence, into the woods, which was forbidden to me, maybe by opening all of the windows I could rid the room of its air.

THE END OF HISTORY

She has more content than she knows what to do with. It is a feeling of being full and unable to find comfort in any position, so she keeps shifting her body, moving it to different rooms in case she might discover in one something also within herself. In her sleep she is also always moving—in the morning she finds the sheets damp and twisted around themselves, as if she is now in a place other than where her body has been resting.

What she wants to discover is a framework for her content, where it will be contained and even put to a good use so that she does not feel she has more than she can manage. There are the lyrics of songs—usually only the chorus—that repeat when she is awake and when she is asleep, occurring in her dreams to different melodies, yet still filling her head with their words. There are actual objects that fill the place where she lives: tables, chairs, the rind of a grapefruit, many plastic bags, dishes with food congealed on their surfaces. There are surfaces, and there are memories of surfaces—the glittering one of the pond where she swam with a man she no longer sees.

She envisions walking into a room—it will be a room in a particular downtown building she has always wanted to enter (she likes the arched shape of its entranceway, which reminds her of a street in a very different city where one night she came across a man weeping beneath a window out of which fell one white sheet, then another white sheet, covering the man's body). Inside the room will be the framework she needs for her content. Yet when she tries to decide what the framework will be made of, she has trouble imagining a structure made by humans that could contain all she has accumulated.

Maybe it will be a hive, or a lattice of crystals. Maybe she will find a space that will be for her content what a greenhouse is for orchids. It will provide just the right conditions for her content to grow and flourish. Her content will send out new shoots, and she will only have to visit occasionally to make sure the correct levels of temperature, moisture, and light are maintaining. Her content will become unruly, and she will not mind. She will not feel overwhelmed by it the way she does now, with no place to put it except to keep carrying it with her all the time, the way a friend once wore a hooded sweatshirt backwards so a stray kitten tucked inside the hood could feel her warmth and hear her voice while she drove the long distances her job required.

She does not know how or why she has acquired so much content—it is just something that happens, it seems, as a result of having a body and senses. Near her apartment there is a fence trash blows against, the trash becoming trapped between the fence and the wind. She thinks of herself as the fence the content has become trapped against. She thinks she might also be the wind.

Reasoning is disastrous because it only seems to generate

more content she doesn't know what to do with. Yet she sometimes thinks that if she were to proceed carefully from one point to the logical next, she could eventually reach a conclusion about her content that would also be a solution to the problem of having too much of it. As far as she can tell, a logical solution to the problem of having too much content would have to negate the content—it would have to be an empty place or an opening that could accommodate all the content she feels burdened by. Since the feeling of being burdened by content is also content, the logical solution will also have to accommodate her feelings, which she doubts a logical solution could ever do. And the solution, also being content, will have to accommodate itself. . . .

As soon as she begins to think like this, she realizes that she is creating more content, and she feels pain in the area of her stomach, as if she has eaten too much. Pain is also content she does not know what to do with.

If she could just find the opening at the end of reason, the small portal or chute she imagines will be there, then she will be able to dispose of her content. She will push it into the small portal or chute and watch it disappear. A breeze will be coming from the portal; she will push her content through the portal and then a breeze will lift the ends of her hair, and she will feel she's speeding along in a convertible, free of history.

She has read about the end of history. While she isn't sure exactly what it means, *the end of history*, she imagines that after it happens, everyone will walk around as if they've just woken up from a nap—hair will be disheveled, eyes puffy, clothing wrinkled. Everyone will be thirsty and wanting to talk about their dreams, which will have become too vague to be narrated.

She does not want to believe in transcendence or happy endings since beliefs, too, are content, so she decides instead to try to shed her content *moment by moment*, in a manner she has heard some people are able to effect by never moving or opening their eyes for days and even months of their lives. In this way, closed off to new content, she might be able to shed what she has accumulated.

One night, after a day of sitting very still and trying not to open her eyes, she dreams she has become trapped in an image. The inside of the image looks like a dilapidated, empty factory building. She keeps moving from large empty room to large empty room, having to walk around wide pillars that keep the image from collapsing beneath the extent of its emptiness. Finally she encounters an old woman sitting at a desk in one of the rooms. She approaches the old woman and asks her how to get out of the image. The old woman nods kindly and points to an elevator shaft. She thanks the old woman, goes to the elevator shaft, steps in, begins falling. As she falls, she sees floor after floor flash by. When she looks in the direction she's falling, she sees a small, square opening stippled with many lights. As she gets closer to the opening, she can also see the spiral shapes of galaxies. She becomes anxious about the opening—she is falling into outer space, she realizes, and she is sure she will not survive. Yet the moment she passes out of the shaft, she is overcome by a feeling of great relief, which acts as a parachute for her falling body—now she is free to float for eternity. Suddenly frightened by the thought of eternity, she wakes herself from the dream.

Since even in dreams she cannot help but see and hear and have new experiences, she does not understand the point of going around with her eyes closed. As long as she has a mind, and senses connected to it, she will be unable to stop taking in the sights, sounds, feelings, odors, and flavors of her surroundings, and from these sensations her mind will be unable to stop inventing the stories and ideas that occur to her one after the next, often so quickly that she has not finished making sense of one before the next comes, then the next, until she is confused and wants to cover her life with a bandage, or one of the white sheets that fell on the weeping man.

You should come with me to aikido, one of her friends says. She does not want to go, yet she goes. During class, she feels like a ghost that has been given a body it does not yet know how to move. Bumping around inside of the body, wearing floppy white clothes, she adjusts the arms and legs in the ways a small, serious man tells her to, but the movements do not feel right. Later, when she is home and out of the floppy clothes, she sees in the mirror many small green bruises on the arms and legs, which are once again her own.

Learn to use your mind's energy against itself, and your mind will stop tormenting you, her friend has said, but in her friend's voice she hears the voice of the small, serious man, whom she does not think of as her friend.

Besides: to learn to use her mind's energy against itself, she would have to add new content. Even if it was content that might eventually ease the burden of having content, at this point, she is so overwhelmed with the content she already has, she thinks she cannot take on any new content even if it's promised that the new content will help her. It all just seems like more advertising.

Instead, she would like to build a factory for her content—a place where her content will be used as quickly as she accumulates it. She thinks of the memory of the pond, of how she and the man she no longer sees finally decided that they were unable, because of their different bodies and perspectives, to see the same glittering surface—this will all be fodder for the content factory, where the creations of an evanescent world will be discorporated. Everything she experiences will feed the content factory's machines, which will turn it all into a mist too vague to be held or remembered. Eventually the machines will have nothing but themselves to feed on, and they'll become mist, too.

I CARRIED MY COMA

At the party for my friend's photograph, "What should become visible?" a woman who was asked her age asked.

Outside, I drank with a group of masks. Each one represented a different death.

"This was his mother, supposed to be. I don't really think of her as a she," a woman said through a grizzly mask.

A man, a lioness, said, "If I made my father, I'd do something like this." He turned away from us.

I followed a path that led to a long wait. At the end would be my friend, signing his name on another man's face. The man lay on a couch beneath a photograph of his wife. The place where the man lay was cold. There, people rode trains to a hole their country made them dig, then rode trains to the place where their country made them live.

I walked away from the wait to an edge of where I lived. I tried to imagine what held it in place holding me all night from behind.

At a nearby pier, a cruise ship littered light. A woman wearing the word SECURITY was patrolling there.

"When I was in a coma," she said, "I wore a fanny pack. I carried my coma around with me. I wanted to keep it close to my body."

"What did it look like?"

She picked something from a plant that began inside the edge and ended in the cruise ship's light. "Kind of like this," she said, "warm and wrapped. I knew I was inside it, so I wanted it near me."

She put the thing from the light in my hand. It was white and fuzzy and seamed, about to hatch.

"Do you want it back?"

"I want you to have something to keep," she said. On her neck, the light from the cruise ship looked like bruises.

I put what she'd given me in a bag I'd borrowed for the night. After it was in there I was more conscious of the strap, how it crossed my body behind my body.

When I got back to the group, I wanted them to ask me where I'd been. Instead, they had found a hole and were taking turns looking in.

I waited for a long time for my friend, but he didn't try to find me, and I didn't try to find him.

+

To get home, I had to drive the highway. In the changing shapes of what was strewn along the shoulder, I was aware of the bag on the seat beside me. I had driven far to borrow it, and while I drove, I had imagined I was my friend. I would see how it hung like my body from my body.

I would try to keep other things between my friend and my body. We were most comfortable together in winter. Carrying those layers was a job to have in common.

We'd met through people between us. I had whispered to a woman's earring, "Meet me outside by the fountain." It was one thing laid in something else, laid in itself again, maybe bone.

To meet me, he'd borrowed someone's coat. I'd watched his face for skin. Inside the coat he was small while we talked. He could make me see that I was watching him.

With one hand driving, I reached into the bag and took out what the woman had given me. I rolled down a window and threw the thing she'd given me at one of the shapes by the shoulder.

When I got out of the car at home, I saw the dark shape I'd sweated into the upholstery. Peel it off and take it to him, I thought.

+

Months later, I saw the woman from that night at another party. When I talked to her, something on her began beeping.

"My mother," she said. "Her meds."

We went outside and stood on a driveway.

"I don't want to go back to the party," I said. "It's strange seeing you again." Though I'd called him, I hadn't seen my friend since the night of his party.

"Where do you want to go instead?"

When we got to the end of the driveway, she was beeping again.

"Do you live with your mother?" I asked.

"I live in one half, she lives in the other," she said. "Sometimes we talk to each other across the middle."

"I couldn't live with my mother," I said.

"Why not?"

"Because she's dead," I said.

Then I said, "Sorry."

+

We walked until we couldn't see the lights from the party.

Though it was dark, I knew something large was beside us, and I thought of the woman who became convinced she was living on top of a huge body of water. She wanted to dig a hole to see the enormity of what she knew was below her. She was old, so she found someone who would dig for her. Her nephew began digging one morning, and before the day was over, the woman was dead. Her family buried her in the hole. It was just the right size for her body.

"Let's go a little farther," I said.

Soon we saw lights again. They were for a different party.

SURROGATE

When I am alone, I scrape at my back and arms with my fingernails. A residue of dead skin accumulates under them. I look at it under my fingernails and pick it out, placing the crusts in a hill beside me. In the universe, mine are statistically insignificant activities, but in the attic, where I am nobody, the little hill I've worked free of my body can be most satisfying to look at again and again, and then to flush down the toilet.

My roommate, Shelia, has been trying to get impregnated. She doesn't like men or doctors, but she still wants a baby. Our friend Dan agreed to help her. It's winter, so he has a lot of free time. I hear him grunting in there with Sheila. Once in a while he comes out, butters his hands with margarine and a spatula, and goes back in.

At night, diamonds stitch themselves in the sky above our house, which is on a slant, and glow. There are power lines, and floods in late May, and the north winds, which are my cousins, always blow.

She's too slippery, and then she isn't slippery enough, and then she's hungry, says Dan. He and I are seeing man-to-man, except that I am not a man. Dan does not know this. All Dan sees is sperms not getting to Sheila's egg. The egg is big and floating in destiny. Destiny is made of tiny crystals, each one unique.

There are now more images in the world than sperms. That's difficult for a man, not that I would know.

Dan also sees: cut grass, cut grass not lifted. He is in landscaping. Grass never cut, stubbed cut grass, overgrown. He runs his hands across the land he's seeing while he talks to me, or maybe it's Sheila's body he's imagining mown.

I am someone who is secretly a bird conversation at 7 a.m. Secretly also I am nobody, as well as rain falling gently on the roof when I am in the attic, where I hide. Up here, in the right kind of light, I easily become the empty spaces. The right kind of light is light without roommates in it.

+

North winds blow. I am in the attic. Below, I hear Dan on Sheila, Sheila on Dan, Sheila and Dan beside each other. I hear the break for margarine. I hear Dan create a sound with his lips that makes the last dead leaves fall from the trees. Brace yourself now. Back into the bedroom. In the wind the diamonds glow. I know the magic of a desolate road, it is the only magic I know, la la.

+

I have always tried falling out of the world whenever I have been in it. It effects such paltry objects to contain me—uncomfortable clothing and conversations, hours, days. In the attic I have bare energy. Bare energy is the kind of energy that makes you like an owl flying past another owl. You look into the other owl's eyes and see nothing, no recognition; you might as well never have happened. Bare energy is the kind that sits in the attic for hours listening to the house ticking in its history, which goes down a ways into the ground and then stops. Where the house's history stops, that's where hell begins, maybe. That's how it is around here, and the north winds.

Will there be a baby? Sheila licks her lips and turns the page. But the baby catalog is empty, full of blanks. She sighs. Can you believe this shit, she says. Somebody must have been having a bad day.

She throws the catalog into the recycling. Later I take it out. On the cover it says LONG SHADOWS. Instead of the baby catalog, they sent her the summer shadow catalog. Oh well. Maybe I'll buy a shadow and keep it in the attic. On Whitsun night we'll dance like goats.

I built a thing in my room that would control the whole universe, Dan tells me. It had gyroscopes and magnets. I told a friend who liked the Lone Ranger that I could make silver bullets with my chemistry set. I spent an hour trying, and he finally turned and said, I don't think you can make silver bullets after all.

+

I order a shadow for Dan. These days spent impregnating Sheila are long ones for a landscaping man. Sometimes at night after I have been in the attic I descend from my lofty height and have beers with him. We stand at the window, talking to our sparkling reflections beyond which the snow. The darkness. The utter uncertainty of life for Dan.

What if she expects me to give the kid money? Dan asks his reflection.

Did you make a contract first? I ask Dan's reflection. Parts of me are fleeting. I am recovering from not existing in the attic.

Like a prenup?

Prenup—the word makes me think of a baby koala or one of those dogs with a smashed face that drools on itself. I want to say to Dan, *I do not know what a prenup is, for I am enchanted, I live under a mountain in the land of forgotten things.*

Mountains, I am from beyond them.

Yeah, I say, like a prenup.

No, I mean we talked. I think we're on the same page. But . . .

Darkling pine needles tinkle their frozen symmetries at us; white billows rise from the souls of houses; an owl flies by on its way to the land of forgotten things.

Did you see that? I ask Dan's reflection.

But boredom has caused Dan's reflection to walk away. Or maybe it's fatigue. I find him lying faceup on the divan. I never used to say *divan* until I lived with Sheila. She also says *spangles*, I can't remember in what context, but she says it a lot. I think it makes her sound patriotic, like a trumpet waving a flag o'er the land of the mutely enraged.

Prenup prenup prenup, I say to Dan with my face very close to his nose. But he is asleep. There is already drool coursing out of him on its way to a sunny pasture where cows are grazing in summer. I consider straddling him and trying out a few of my moves, but I don't. I go back up to the attic. I dance even though I haven't got a shadow. Above me the ceiling endlessly peaks, like a mountain climbing itself triumphantly, glad because it is not a man.

CELL FISH

He shook the bag onto the table but something stayed inside. I had the feeling he wasn't telling me some things.

"What's in the bag?"

"What?"

Earlier we watched a documentary about people who live in tunnels. One man had built a tunnel from his kitchen to a nearby country so that he could buy cigarettes and guns. He said that when he walked on the street, he imagined falling, the ground caving where he knew it was thinnest, and dust.

We were inside a tiny Mexican restaurant finishing a meal. A man blew smoke out of two holes. An exhaust fan sounded like bagpipes.

+

We took the boat and were on the lake all day. The water had recently thawed and was still cold; if I put my hand under for long enough, my body would forget my hand.

I put my hand that my body had forgotten on his forehead. He was getting sick or the sky had never been that green, milk torn out of a leaf.

He asked for the aloe because he was burning. As I passed him the aloe he let go of the oar. He slumped forward and I noticed that the moon was rising. I held the aloe toward the moon.

+

"I'm afraid," the doctor said, "he's very sick." I could see the moon through her window. Outside it wasn't dark, yet when I projected my life ten minutes into the future, everything appeared dark and flat, like a screen after a movie based on someone else's life.

He was lying on a gurney somewhere in a room where he couldn't see the moon. The inside of his body was exposed on a technician's screen.

One time when he and I were having sex, I tried to think of the inside of him. I thought of fluids being squeezed through tight, muscular cavities. It seemed crowded in there, and when I felt his body flex against me, there was no space for me.

On the technician's screen, the inside of him looked like the entrance to a cave or a long hallway.

I'm afraid of him, I thought. I thought of us having sex that night and me falling into him, slipping into a space I would have to travel.

The doctor pressed her fingertips together, enclosing the space in front of her face. When she spoke, her voice seemed to come from the space enclosed by her hands.

She said something about seeing. Would he lose his vision? "Wait," she said, "what am I forgetting?" She dropped her hands.

When I noticed that she was wearing a mood ring, I was able to open up.

+

I was telling him about himself. "The doctor said . . ."

He turned away from me so he faced a wall. We were in our bedroom. The petals on the flowers on the wallpaper seemed too thick. Every decorative thing seemed freakish now that he was sick, and everything looked decorative, a length of ribbon tied to a fan.

In a store that sold appliances, I tried to think of one cell making copies of its walls. I thought of a tiny cell within that cell, and then a tinier cell within the tiny cell, all the way down. This illustrated why he was getting thinner. He was caving in.

+

I took our boat out every morning. Something in the water communicated something to the air so that the two remained separate, though mornings they were a little mixed together, and fog rippled below each stroke of my oar, and water collected in the part of my hair.

Summer got hotter. I was getting stronger. Fish swam to the surface of the water early in the morning, then down to where it was dark when the sun reflected on the water. Everything I looked at seemed to be hiding a lot of activity, as if what I saw were just outer walls. When I poked a fish floating belly-up with my oar, a smaller fish swam slowly out.

I rowed to what I thought was the center of the water. When I got there I thought, *This must be the center*, because I'd just had the idea to take off all of my clothes and sit on them to keep from getting splinters.

When I was naked, I thought, *I'm probably the strongest I've ever been.* The sun was bright and felt good on my skin. I was looking at the smoothness of a muscle in my forearm. Just then a fish leaped out of the water and over the front of my boat. I could see each scale, and I could also see the fish. I looked around me. My boat had not gone anywhere but I had gone somewhere and come back.

+

"I caught a fish," I told him. After I'd gone to the center and back, I tied up the boat and put on my clothes, took out his fishing pole and lure and fished from the dock. It took a long time to lure a fish from the dark under the surface, exactly as much time as it had taken the sun to go from noon to behind the tall pines.

"What kind of fish is it," he asked. I could see him breathing. He wasn't wearing a shirt and his chest was thin and the skin at his neck fluttered like he was breathing through it.

"I don't know," I said. I held it up. It was dead, but when it was still moving I had grabbed it with my hands, though I didn't like how it felt to hold something that was fighting against me.

"It isn't a bass," he said, "but it's still big."

"Are you hungry?" I asked. He moved his mouth.

+

He had stopped eating but he was still moving his mouth. He had hardly eaten. His bones looked like a raft of lashed sticks. A bird landed a short distance from our table.

On the table, pushed to an edge, was a pile of bills from the doctor.

"I'm afraid for you," I told him, "but also for myself."

He wanted to know what the doctor had told me on the phone. While she talked to me I looked out to the water because that was the biggest thing I could see; I wanted the water to cancel something out.

When I looked at the table my eyes went right to a knot in the wood. "I don't remember," I lied to him.

I looked up in time to see the bird carrying away a spine. That was the last of our fish.

"I'm going to make us dessert," he said.

+

I waited a long time at the table, and then I walked to the dock. I waited until the sky was completely dark and the moon was a sliver in it, and then I walked back to the house.

He had scooped ice cream into bowls and the ice cream had melted. I felt one of the bowls and it wasn't cold. Everything had evened out. I didn't feel so strong. The light in the room was off. I heard his breath and felt something soft around my neck.

THE ART TEACHER

When she took her students to see the trash heap at the museum, they did not come to any conclusions. Nothing seemed locked to its meaning the way the things they were used to were used to seeming. An old armchair crawled across the dainty fading of its upholstery and fainted. A love seat just sort of floated above some sneakers that seemed to be in charge of their own bright insignias and soles, ordering them to grow a flashy green mold in retaliation against the museum's dull white walls. Nobody knew what was the artist's goal; not even the artist did, according to a pamphlet. It seemed, perhaps, that visitors were meant to steal from the heap's proliferating images, and so she told her students to steal, which they did, gleefully, from the museum.

She abandoned them to their theft and found a bench in the Baroque wing; there the meaning of things was clear and easy to see: she was tired of teaching and policing; she wanted to escape through the seams of her identity into a dream of something else, or somebody. Once she had dreamed that she was a plant owned by a widow who kept her in a tiny pot that she would water from a cracked teacup each morning; the teacup leaked all its water before it could reach her pot, yet she found an internal way to survive, growing a toughened stalk. Another time, she had been a man who, to maintain the integrity of his identity, found a way to make more of himself without sex, which demanded a fusion he found terrifying and cold. She had liked the feeling of being contained by the tiny pot—it was exactly the same feeling she'd had when she had been the man. She longed to return to that feeling now, when she felt her identity perforated, like a wall for windows, or no, like a wall of a museum, a different, framed rendering for each child she was supposed to oversee.

One, an undersized child who had been renamed Lawrence to help him grow, began crying through his nose. Clear water flowed from his nostrils down to his clothes and continued to flow, seeking paths of less resistance toward more of its own, finally emptying its identity—by now it had been named the Lawrence River—into the ocean.

Or no, Lawrence just had a runny nose. She apologized to the child for having called him a river.

+

At night, she went home, where there weren't any students, and felt cold. She had a small instrument for sensing things; she would lay herself across it without any goal. She did not know how to play the instrument or even whether it could be played. By then it would be very late, so late it would be the next day, and she would rise from her life and go to school.

It was a body, she thought, or it was a tool.

+

Sometimes it was difficult to find the school—it disguised itself to evade its own authority, which was crippling it from the inside out, she was told in a memo delivered to her by a man she recognized as the school's vice-principal.

He arrived at her door one morning. "Hal?" she said.

But the man only tipped a hat that he wasn't even wearing— he hadn't tipped a thing, yet he acted so corny, as if he imagined himself an actual renegade, as if any change could come of *imagining* a renegade.

Less and less, she trusted the imagination. One morning, wandering the periphery of a trash-strewn man, she recognized the man as one of her students, the one who had been Lawrence, and she resolved not to waste any more time, which was passing faster than ever.

She decided to buy a bicycle. She had seen people riding upon the look they got in their eyes when they talked about their bikes—on their pupils these people would float up and up until they were enveloped in the shiny white cloud of their mind as they tried to fit a feeling of freedom into words.

"You know, it's like, green?" they would say, and they would say "vvvrrrrooooooooom" to indicate the dealing of wind with the convolutions of the ear canal.

From such conversations she managed to enact a sense of what riding a bicycle was like once she had one of her own. She decided that riding it was like being her own home. She looked out of her own face at the way things disappeared as she zoomed past, felt with her own wind the porousness of her skin. But this was just the beginning of freedom; soon she needed a way to make money because riding a bicycle made her very hungry.

+

She decided to acquire students. This time, though, she would not trouble herself with confusing institutions. She would not try to pass herself off as proficient. She would not shower, or put on a shirt that revealed her. She would not rub her armpits against a deodorant trinket. She would not develop tension in her neck by trying to smile with her eyes. Instead she would just ride.

In the streets, an animal like a tiny deer had for years been shedding its antlers into the spaces that were widening between everything and its meaning. They weren't even antlers anymore—proprietors were selling them as trinkets; others were selling them as floss. She didn't know how to account for the loss of the antlers as antlers; didn't people hear the tiny deer that clicked past? She heard them bounding with tinkling purpose, like broken glass being gathered by smashed vessels slowly taking back their shapes.

Yet once their antlers-as-antlers had disappeared, the deer were denied; they had never been alive.

Meanwhile, the widening was accepted as fact: when pavement cracked or a lot got vacant, spaces pushed in to take their place among the city's edifices, as if emptiness were also constructed. In these spaces there soon grew plants and trees with lavish leaves and possibly medicinal properties, so people put snacks into backpacks and wandered off into new wildernesses, hoping to find beauty, mystery, and to get high. It was said that breakthroughs in understanding the human psyche were on their way, but mostly people just got lost until they found their way back onto a map of the city's commercial districts.

The city had begun calling these inexplicable gaps in its carefully planned surfaces "green spaces," for spaces they obviously were, and green they could sometimes be, though it was obvious that *green* was being used as a metaphor for wildness and unpredictability and everything else that threatened the business of the city.

But her business was now separate from the city's; having nearly no money, she did not feel she had to hurry. She rode her bicycle slowly, letting her legs be a ladder that supported the weight of others, should any others care for a ride. She connected a carriage to her rear axle and this added considerably to the work she had to do to propel her entire life forward, but nobody seemed to find this annoying, especially not her. Soon the extra weight was added to by bodies—two women who did not wear shoes and who entwined themselves madly in each other's charms.

She wondered what new aspects of herself she might see while she towed these women through the city. What she found was that she had a habit of looking for approval to the surfaces of the city that gleamed maniacally at the skyline. Yet she herself was perfectly capable of being her own home.

She knew this.

"I'm tired of whatever it is I'm looking for," she said to the women one day while they stopped for a pistachio-coconut shake. The women were positioned in the carriage so that they appeared to be a single woman with an extra shake.

"Come in here with us," they said, bobbing their embrasured head.

"Do you mean that metaphorically?" she asked. Yet it was obvious that their togetherness was a tunnel for them, a real recess away from the day of the world of the city, and within it they were happy and shady.

"Yes," they said.

+

She slept especially well after long rides—she barely even felt her instrument as she drifted into it, across it. Whatever the instrument was—lovers had tried to discover her memory of its name—she couldn't say. She felt it was a physical thing. She actually felt ill when she tried to decide what the instrument was, or wasn't. It had its own softness, its own lost context that gave it, in the context of her bedroom, its opacity. Who knew where the instrument was from, where it was going? Certainly it seemed to be on its way somewhere, for when she lay across it in her underwear, she could feel where it had begun to disappear into the grayness of the underlying carpet.

She did have a few memories that perhaps pertained to the origin of the instrument. For instance, there was the man who carried a land shape. A peninsula, most likely, since it seemed to be connected to his body, though she had always liked the idea that it was an island and that he, like the tide, was simply overlapping it.

And there was the woman who had a drumbeat. She had a rhythm in her skin, and a rhyme besides. The woman was someone she had once been inside; she had lived with the woman in her skin. Eventually, as with all rhythms, there had been an end. She had left the woman, yet something of her rhythm remained, as in the way a day fades into a day.

And so the instrument remained, and now it too had begun to fade.

+

Each day was a true consequence of her decision to live. There were plenty of ways to lie; after we close our eyes, she read in a science magazine, an illusion persists for sometimes our whole life.

With respect to her eyes, she could often see the yellow slide in the park across the street from her apartment; children would tumble from one end of it, having come from somewhere else. She could not see where they came from; it was a long slide, its origins concealed in the leaves of trees above it and to either side.

And so the children came from somewhere beyond her

control or permission and landed at the bottom of the slide, within her sight; once there, each child unknowingly became her student. Her lesson was that she was there to see them, whomever they may be.

Sometimes she was surprised by what came out of the slide; sometimes, things weren't alive.

+

Watching the slide, she would stand in her window and drink coffee; this was how she taught. Then she would get onto her bike.

She biked along a continuum from doom to seven: doom was starting out sore and early; by seven in the evening, she could decide to feel alright. By then she would be carrying the sun in her skin; it made her happy to feel the sun evaporating from her back, returning to the air where it could darken the sky. She was fine with night. It steamed off her back after a ride, when her skin would glisten with the moon already beginning to rise. And if there was to be no moon that night? She would still feel her skin tightening around the vastness she had traveled that day. In the same way, the stars tightened in their shine, as the dark around them knew, and became harder, too.

+

She became strong. Day after day she rode slowly through the latitudes of the city. One begins as a student but becomes a friend of clouds, she thought. Mine is an art that is inseparable from the search for reality.

When she needed rest, she would bike into a green space and lie back on the unsanctioned grass. It grew with illicit speed, according to the city; it could not be made to look cute or tame, like something one would want to name or fuck—it grew wildly and unpredictably, each tuft aswirl with its own microclimate. No one had designed this strategy of the grass's to grow wherever and however it wanted, and so it was seen as a menace to the patented genetic identities of subsidized crops. Corporate corn growers were quick to elect a wall to the borderlands of the city; through the wall's oversight, the city became an ancient citadel that languished at all hours but those few each evening when, revived by a shared memory of the coming night, people of the city would quickly leave their domiciles to acquire rough cuts of meat and to fill their bottles with mead, or something—they didn't really know what the brown sludge was. Some people called it mead and so other people, not knowing what mead was, called it mead, too.

On certain holidays, a person was allowed to walk the promenade atop the city's wall, and to marvel at the unendingness of sight—how it found so many examples of the same species to pack into a glance. There was corn upon corn, stretched to the horizon and growing *on* the horizon—it wasn't any trouble after all to graft corn to the illusory line made by the limit of the eye's might.

The fact that all limits had been surpassed was the occasion for a holiday. Wasn't it golden, that fact? Didn't it possess measurable mass, wasn't it the being one could see through the windows of the black, bulletproof sedan that rolled up and down the rows of corn, crushing them? Wasn't destruction, when done by fact, simply a fact, and therefore beyond command?

She did not answer any of these questions that weren't questions but holes being shrugged casually into language. She did not want to make any of them seem deep.

+

Lately she felt herself to be on the verge of a monument, nearing the center of being found. Here I am, she wanted to say to everybody, as if to reassure them that a terrible contagion had been contained.

When there wasn't much left of the instrument, she bought a potted plant to replace it. The plant grew into a room where she could sit to admire it. She liked the way its flower followed noon, finding it in the morning on one side of the sky and following it all the way to another day. What would happen if another day never came? The flower would find a way, she imagined, to drag it out of the sky.

Also, she couldn't not imagine the utter hiss of final darkness.

+

One night, from the vantage of her continuum, she could see an end to it.

She had walked her bike onto the promenade at the top of the wall, violating a sign.

Someone was sitting there, and she knew it was him: Hal, the vice-principal.

What a strange way to return to a place I've never been, she thought as she approached him, not quite sure what this meant.

He sat with a cowboy on his lap. No, the cowboy was his hat, but in the shadow it cast below the wall, she saw its boots.

"I'm going over the side," he said. "Other than that, I don't know who I'll shoot." When he leaped, Hal would land in the boots of his hat.

EVERY DAY, AN EPIC

Every day a tide rolls up to beauty and convulses it. This means I have been reading. I have been looking at the world through a lens. I have been looking through the lens and I have been looking out around its edges and it is there, where no lens extends, that I see:

and I enter into it. I enter into an agreement to be contained by it. Could it come up to my knees with its absences and lands? Could it rock and drag the clouds from one side of the sky to my open hand? It can and I am ready. I will eat three continuities and they will be lambs. They will be hillsides and they will be spilling. Then they will be green and I will have recovered from them.

I have already recovered. I am inside a man. I am wearing beige and it is raining. This is how I can stand it: I can't. I leave immediately. I open intervals and unravel across them. I leave many strings dangling but no connecting edge, nothing to come to when I'm confused, nowhere to stand to say, This is where I stand; beyond this I do not stand. I have nowhere like sand, or a leap, or a mountain. Briefly I inhabit the shape of *fountain*: I lose my head. I toss across a clean outcrop of marble. My body could be made in its veins. There it might take the shape of a woman as she is imagined by a man, by a history, as she tries to escape from a maze. Her center will be the same as her surface: me. I am spreading rapidly. Every day I am a fish before I am forgotten. Then I am a surge. I rush from a word toward its object with my great capacity for love. Can I love whatever it is I am coming to, even if it turns out to be crumbling? What if, in my rush, I discover that I prefer the rush to the object, the rush to the world? Then I am the death-driver, I am the lightning bolt tattoo zapping the skull tattoo, I annihilate all silver and crystal and mothers and sons, I am an arrow leaving the sun and annihilating the sun, an all-in-one unto no one but one: a much older woman named Melt. She wants me to call her Melt, so I perform vertiginously upon her body with my shoe, then with my bare hands. When I don't know what else to do, I do headstands and supra-headstands, meaning I leap out of my skull and show her my tattoo. She shows me her own body. It is as real as a peninsula and as tan. It contains the generation known as Man. She and I get along quietly and then all of a sudden we do not get along at all, I am tossed from her rocks and her cliffs and her hands into a depth of myself that I cannot stand. It is simply skin, this borderland, yet I cannot get beyond it. But what is beyond it? There must lie the self: the possibility of someone else. Let me see who she is, or he: a farmer, a doctor, a neighbor, a bakery? A very large purse stuffed with stolen prescription pills? What else could the self be if not possibility? Beyond this, there must lie the shelf: the sand. I will swim from these hands into former hands, forms I have had and might have again if I can be gentle in how I go about this, brushing softly the entire length of the cat. Briefly a self forms in sense contact. Then

I stiffen and sneeze. So I am real, then—I am a cat. Yet I have often crept beyond these boundaries—I have slept. No matter what form it takes, the sea does not soothe one in sleep. Either the movement is excessively vast or my body surpasses an avalanche in its power to displace, so I wake. I swim the liquid waves of Neptune. Trees traverse the sea in the form of boats: fir oars sweeping waves, pine timbers fitting to the wind's curved keel. Emerging from the eddies I am visible as far as breasts, nakedness. It's true I'm on a quest to discover what I am. Yet it plays out in ordinary ways. I jog. I take cash out of a machine, and it's as if money has value, like breath and "Good job!" Yet from the ground it is difficult to see the overall pattern. Often my path is guided only by impulse—suddenly I see a certain quality of green and know that any way I choose to go is already known— but if not by me, then by what extension of my breath? For when I arrive I see that I am nowhere really: I see the chair where I am still sitting, admiring the apparition of home. The ivory of the chairs gleams white, the cups of the table shine, the whole house rejoices with the glittering royal treasure. I extend as far back as royal opulence goes, then put on my clothes. Time to leave again. But where will I go? Looking out from the wave-resounding shore, bearing uncontrollable furies in my heart, I do not even believe that I see what I see.

4 STORIES

AN ADVENTURE STORY

A point begins moving in a direction, trailing a line behind it. The line is a record and describes: Here is, was, and will be again, in time.

If a good adventure story is a trajectory, and a measure of the heroism extolled within it a function of how far and through how difficult a landscape the trajectory travels from the point where the trajectory begins, then by this measure, this adventure story is not a good one: it doubles back around the middle, then doubles back again, and stays there, circling an indistinct figure.

The figure is standing knee-deep in snow, or the figure is drowning.

In order to reach this figure and save it, the story casts off its unnecessary weight. It casts off its characters, who are weak, pale, and heavy, a family of four. It casts off its narrator, who is prone to exaggeration. It casts off details that do not add to its forward momentum, but in doing this, it has made an error: because the story is circling, forward momentum only increases the sensation of centrifugal force, which pushes the story away from its object.

In its haste to save the figure, the story has furthered the distance between the figure and itself, and continues spinning in ever-widening circles, powerless to stop in this fictitious, frictionless landscape.

Meanwhile, the narrator, who feels disillusioned with the story and everything the story does, goes on a long walk by herself, and becomes lost.

THE PHEASANT AND THE FUNGUS[1]

Each time the door is opened, a wedge of orange light overlaps the faint circle of yellow cast by the streetlight. Inside, diners are seated at two long tables that extend back past the kitchen to the other end of the restaurant, which lies in a far quadrant of the night. Diners are dressed beautifully, in hats and dresses and suits and scarves, and sit waiting with extreme patience, for they have an extreme zeal for patience. Perhaps it is this zeal that brings them night after night to the restaurant, with its simple wooden tables and benches, its plain though expensive meals, and a view of the kitchen where the cook works. The cook wears a red stocking cap and looks like someone who was once shipwrecked, lost at sea, and navigated home by the stars, and she can be seen tirelessly preparing in tall copper pots and cast-iron skillets what once lived blithe and uncaring in the forest.

Along the benches, couples seated across from one another lean forward in order to hold conversations about beekeeping, shipbuilding, and the mechanical genius of the astrolabe.

Yes, we have to divide up our time like this. The whole visible world is perhaps nothing other than a motivation of our wish to rest for a moment.

Before the meal is served, the cook comes out of the kitchen, and standing on a chair, says, "I want to thank you for the great confidence you have placed in me. That is all I can do. I do not believe that man is a useless passion. The quest for the marvelous does not end, for being itself is this quest." The cook returns to the kitchen, and the diners soon find their plates full, their minds empty.

IDEAS ABOUT THEM[2]

Fatigue comes from them. The wearing out of the clothes of scholars is due to their rubbing against them. The opaqueness in the eyes of the blind is their reflection. Each mirror is one hallway of their chamber. When you shiver, it is because they are behind you. A sigh is their minor accompaniment. A scream is their primary abode. A cloud to them is just as loud. A malady their four-leafed clover. When the door's hinges wail, it is because they have been through. The bruising of the feet comes from them. One who paces walks beside them. In hesitation they live their entire lives.

If one wants to discover them, or to speak of them among a crowd, let him come to harm. Let him, however prayed-for, arrive at harm, and be removed to one of harm's wards. Let the children of harm cobble him shoes with which to walk through harm. Let him, one afternoon when he believes he has escaped harm, fall to his knees, and die. Then he will see them, and he will speak with them of nothing, for that is all they speak of.

We welcome them. We go through them like light through film, and they watch us, offering no help.

AN EXAMPLE OF SINGLE-MINDEDNESS

When he was a boy, his influence on the world seemed calculable: there was the island, and it took X number of strokes of a paddle of Y length to reach it. There were enough hours in the part of the day he was allowed to inhabit—the part that began with the sound of a dish in the kitchen, a woman calling his name, and ended with the sound of a dish in the kitchen, the woman calling a man's name—for him to make Z number of trips to the island, each trip ferrying a squirrel he had trapped in his father's trap. His intelligence was circumscribed only by wonder, and by the number of hours he was allowed to inhabit each day. From his bed before he slept, before the light had completely faded, he watched the island through binoculars, believing, It won't be long now, it won't be long now, it won't be long now.

Now, when I look out my window at a certain time of day, I see him pass by on his bicycle, riding up the hill. He has a silly grin on his thin face and in the leathery pouch affixed to his handlebars he carries something for the one who waits at the top of the hill. My house is only halfway.

—

1. "The Pheasant and the Fungus" makes use of the following sources:

Einstein, Albert. "Yes, we have to divide up our time like that, between our politics and our equations."

Kafka, Franz. "The whole visible world is perhaps nothing more than the rationalization of a man who wants to find peace for a moment."

Michau, Michael R. "On Escape." *Other Voices: the (e)Journal of Cultural Criticism*, v. 2., no. 3 (January 2005).

Rilke, Rainer Maria. *Letters to a Young Poet*. "I want to thank you for the great confidence you have placed in me. That is all I can do."

2. The first two lines of "Ideas About Them" are from a folktale about Mazikin, a kind of demon thought to inhabit a realm just beyond the visible. Found in *The Hebrew Folktale* by Eli Yassif (author), Jacqueline S. Teitelbaum (translator), pages 145–146.

SAG: A SAGA

We lived in a valley of glacial till, a morass of moraine arranged by chance, as was my wedding to a man whose life was easy and brief, given up to the gods of excess and paunch.

He would go and come back, come back distant, then come back from his coming back angry. If I could watch myself from outside our window pry off his finger . . . I often would think, but thinking is no window. Now I think less of thinking. I have broken windows.

+

We were married in a garden of stone, few flowers, fewer hours each day after, until darkness was our only and every hour, and every light in our home had to be brightly on. There was something I suppose the matter with his vision— he saw far, but only into himself, where he found himself looking back and laughing.

He was innocent in his proportions and in his distress. He preferred linen suits that were loose so that he could sweat unrestricted. He was huge but could not grasp himself. He emptied books of their meaning as he tried to reach through them to himself, though often he just threw the books back at the shelf. He thrashed in our brightly lighted bedroom at night, drew the white sheets in a swath to his body. He looked like one of those Roman women carved in stone. He looked like one of those emperors who thrashes once and is done.

I am not brutal, he brooded.

+

His head twisted off into the light: our first night together.

My arm I placed in a door. I had hoped an escape was coming. I had thought, Love must be brutal to relieve me.

Love must be gone to leave me.

Love must be a hinged thing so that it slams.

Love must be an ingot so that it may be traded, sold, stored, recast, traded again, resold. It must be common as gold.

He was in the trade of metals. He came from a family that speculated in what was barely beneath the surface.

He hated that history is malleable and can be recast and retold. He worried how it would turn out for himself and his family. He regretted that his one brother was slow. Not retarded, no. But slow to make his millions grow.

+

The slow brother had a telescope and liked to observe the fixed stars.

My husband preferred the gold standard to celestial mechanics.

When the gold standard was abandoned the family managed stakes in silver; when silver tarnished they ored.

Copper or tungsten or nickel. Then crude petroleum.

He thinks too much, the world is too much with him, my husband said of his younger brother, quoting from a book he'd gone through and thrown.

Naturally their business soon was standard gas.

Let there be movement among the heavenly bodies.

A motor spirit put the fixed stars in motion—

+

not perpetual. The wells dried, and there had to be a crash.

After he lost everything the slow brother came to stay with us. My husband left to oversee a trade.

One night this brother pushed on my door. I heard the hinge. I swung open for him. It happened again, and then he left.

By then the hinge was rusted so the door could not slam shut. But he did push it. He pushed it twice.

+

Both of our children were born blue and crooked. It was a matter of their bones having fused in a confusion that is the source of itself. The doctor who pulled them from me would not let me see them, tucking them under his gown. Each child had reached a blue hand out of me and jammed it into the doctor's mouth, a sign of contempt and derision.

Even when they were inside me I could sense them laughing: the first one rattled my bones, the second made me frightened for myself.

My husband did not appear to hear. In a rage one day he had stopped up his ears with wax.

His chiseled features had begun to sag so he covered them with wax.

Has-been, I remember thinking bitterly, sounds a bit like *husband*.

+

There are sources of delight in this language, though no longer in my body: the proximity of caul to cauldron. Our children were born within a year of each other, each born in a caul. The first time I saw my second I thought, My God, he has no face, he has no face! I thought his face must be still inside my body. Right away I went to the ocean. Salt collapses the wall of each cell and what's trapped might escape me, I'd imagined.

I swam out beyond a beyond I had imagined would be a cue, a coming-to of reason embodied in a scream. When I saw his face in a rock on an island I screamed. I returned to find my son grown a man.

My first child had the gall to be a dancer. The river that flowed north past our yard toward the memory of its glacier raged in spring and I believe this rage was what I watched when she was dancing. She found postures that were the postures a body finds in the sinuous act of murder. At least if I were to murder I would hold my neck like that, with an insolent crook society cannot straighten. The crook the river took to carve an escarpment in its route around our home was where I often found her playing with broken toy things and my broom.

+

One afternoon my has-been went inside a room inside the house inside an hour. I watched my daughter launch a leap over the water. From then on there was just his voice occasionally that insisted, Leave the lights on! We did not see him again.

Well, the wind blew, and a city grew in rings around its howl. We watched our lives live themselves as if they were our neighbors, build houses, drive cars into yards. We sat on our weathered porch and were bored, very, by the ongoingness of this projection.

All that's left of our house is a window. There's not even a wall to contain it. My voice that cannot contain this story circles back for its self.

For my next marriage, raiment of ashes.

ACKNOWLEDGMENTS

The author would like to thank the editors of the following publications, in which stories from this collection have appeared: *Attempt Magazine, Beecher's Magazine, Birkensnake, BOMB Magazine, The Collagist, Conjunctions, The Cossack Review, The Fanzine, H_NGM_N, The New Yinzer, Pindeldyboz, Sidebrow,* and *Vestiges.*

Thank you also to the Oregon Health Plan, Medi-Cal, the Supplemental Nutrition Assistance Program, and Brown University for assistance during the years this book was being written.

And deepest thanks to friends and family, most especially Amy, Darcie, Brian, Andrew, Benny, Miranda, Mark, Matthew, and Adam, whose care, patience, and imaginations make everything possible.

Note:

"Jay" includes material found in "A Pickpocket's Tale" by Adam Green (*The New Yorker,* January 7, 2013).

"From Documentary Filmmaker Jurgen Grossbinger's Journal" includes materials from *A Lover's Discourse: Fragments* by Roland Barthers (New York: Hill and Wang, 1978).